Hamba Sugar Daddy

Hamba Sugar Daddy

Nape `a Motana

First published by Jacana Media (Pty) Ltd in 2016

10 Orange Street
Sunnyside
Auckland Park 2092
South Africa
+2711 628 3200
www.jacana.co.za

© Nape `a Motana, 2016

All rights reserved.

ISBN 978-1-4314-2422-1

For the reader's convenience, a glossary appears at the end of the novel

Cover design by Karen Wentzel
Set in Sabon 11/14.5pt
Printed and bound by Shumani Mills Communications, Parow, Cape Town
Job no. 002784

Also available as an e-book:
d-PDF 978-1-4314-2446-7
ePUB 978-1-4314-2447-4
mobi file 978-1-4314-2448-1

See a complete list of Jacana titles at www.jacana.co.za

To my daughters, Thabang and Mmasello, their peers and the born-frees who are faced with pertinent challenges as girl children, who as captains are continuing to steer their ships in especially shark-infested and tempestuous seas, often tasting their own sweat, tears and blood, in an attempt to avoid shipwrecks. My children, according to a Sepedi proverb, Bohlale bo tšwa lebading – *Wisdom comes from the scar.* Tšea o kwe!

PART ONE

1

During break at Solomon Mahlangu High School, the red-brick building comprising several classrooms ejected thousands of boys and girls, wearing blue-and-yellow school uniforms. A loud chatter and bursts of laughter filled the place as the learners shuffled out of the classrooms.

Rolivhuwa Ramabulana, a Grade 12 girl, in eager haste walked past other students and strutted down the stairs of the double-storey building. At the bottom of the steps she paused and looked around. She walked towards a group of five girls standing in a cluster next to a classroom, basking in the winter sun on that first Friday in May; they were chewing what they had already bought from the aunties who hawked peanuts, sweets, apples, pears, sandwiches and other types of cold food preferred by the learners. Rolivhuwa stood right in front of Kedibone Malope, another Grade 12 learner who was in another class.

'*Chomi ya ka*,' said Rolivhuwa, smiling at her target, 'Please lend me another five rand,' Rolivhuwa opened her palm and exposed a five-rand coin, 'so that I can buy *sphatlo*.'

'Roli,' responded Kedibone, 'Are you aware that now you owe me twenty rand?'

'I know, Kedi; my aunt did not have loose money and she was rushing to catch her train. She will give me money tonight, and I will repay you the whole amount on Monday.'

Kedibone took out a coin and handed it to Rolivhuwa who returned a few minutes later and started munching and exchanged friendly glances with Kedibone and other girls.

Kedibone gave Rolivhuwa a naughty smile. 'Roli, I was just telling these girls here that you can use your God-given body to make good pocket money for yourself.'

The other four girls guffawed. Rolivhuwa laughed with them but a moment later she looked down, digesting what Kedibone had just said.

* * *

On Monday morning during break, Rolivhuwa sat alone in her class with an open accounting book in front of her. Her mind was not on the book; she was thinking of the R20 which she owed Kedibone.

'So you are trying to avoid me, Roli?'

Rolivhuwa was dismayed to see Kedibone's stern face.

'I'm not dodging you, Kedi!'

Kedibone smiled sarcastically and stretched out an open palm towards Rolivhuwa who sighed and then buried her face in her hands, embarrassed to make eye contact with her creditor.

'I'm sorry Kedi,' said Rolivhuwa with downcast eyes. 'My aunt has disappointed me. She said she used part of her weekly wages to pay for the arrears of her burial society and that she had to help her colleague who needed money for her mother's funeral.'

'I don't care about burial societies and other people's mother's funerals! All I want is *my* money! When you want me to lend you money you say *chomi ya ka, chomi ya ka*! Listen Roli, if you don't bring my R20 tomorrow, you must forget about our friendship!'

'I'm terribly sorry, Kedi!' said Rolivhuwa softly. 'I'll talk to my mother to make a plan tonight. Please Kedi!'

Kedibone gave her a long hard look before her face broke into a crooked smile.

'I told you that you can use your body,' Kedibone pointed towards Rolivhuwa's well-built thighs, which were habitually exposed by a short skirt and glowed because they were well-maintained with glycerine, in summer and in winter.

Rolivhuwa smiled towards Kedibone. 'Are you serious?'

'Yes!' Kedibone brushed Rolivhuwa's thighs. 'It's a matter of opening your beautiful shiny thighs, and you'll have bank notes transferred into your purse soon!'

Kedibone guffawed.

'I can't be a prostitute, Kedi!' Rolivhuwa protested.

Kedibone chuckled. 'You don't understand, Roli. I'm talking about having a relationship with a man who has money; I mean a stack of money, not a lousy guy who'll tell you about burial societies, mother's funerals and a long list of lame excuses.'

Rolivhuwa gave Kedibone a quizzical grin.

'Let me put it this way,' Kedibone continued, 'the surest way of laughing all the way home with a fat purse and wonderful gifts is to be the rich man's sugar baby.'

'What is a sugar baby?'

'Do you really want to know?'

'Please tell me, Kedi.'

'But why don't you guess what I mean? No, I won't tell you.'

Kedibone stepped out of Rolivhuwa's classroom, laughing loudly as other learners entered at the end of the break.

* * *

The following day during break, Rolivhuwa walked over to Kedibone, repaid her debt and then hurried towards a stall where she bought a sandwich made up of thick slices of a white loaf, *mashangani* wors, eggs and atchar. She looked around before she sauntered towards Khomisa Maluleka, another Grade 12 girl, who was known as the leader of *bazalwane*, the bornagain Christian students. After they had exchanged greetings, Rolivhuwa heard Khomisa praying: *Father I thank You for this food I am about to enjoy and I ask You to bless it, Amen.*

Rolivhuwa smiled and made a face towards Khomisa. 'You can make a perfect *mamfundisi, wena.*'

Khomisa chuckled. 'I take it as a compliment, Roli.'

'It's a compliment, Khomi.'

Rolivhuwa and Khomisa ate as they talked.

'Tell me, Khomi, what is a sugar baby?'

Khomisa kept quiet for a moment. 'I don't know. But I have a feeling that it's something, uhm … not pure, something evil.'

'Something evil?'

'Yes. I think you must ask that group over there that question.'

Khomisa was gesturing towards Kedibone and her friends.

'Why?' inquired Rolivhuwa.

'My Bible tells me that the children of this world are more cunning and shrewd than the children of light.'

'You really speak good English, eh?'

Khomisa chuckled.

Rolivhuwa pointed somewhere. 'Look, Ma'am Legodi is coming. Let's ask her!'

2

'Ma'am,' said Rolivhuwa, 'What is a sugar baby?'

'The term "Sugar baby" falls under the topic: "Age disparity in sexual relationships",' Ms Legodi explained to Rolivhuwa that afternoon.

'What is age disparity, ma'am?'

'It's a wide age difference of perhaps up to 20 years. In this sexual relationship the older is perceived as the richer, and is known as the "sugar daddy", and the younger of the two is called "sugar baby".'

'I see, ma'am.'

'A new breed of sugar daddies are known as blessers; these are usually rich old men who lure young women, shower them with gifts and take them to expensive holiday destinations in exchange for sex and companionships; the women who are blessed are known as blessees.'

Ms Legodi looked at her with curiosity. 'Where did you hear about this expression?'

'From a women's magazine, ma'am.'

'I just want to warn you against bad company, Roli,' said Ms Legodi. 'According to HIV/AIDS and gender experts and activists, sugar daddies who promise young girls easy money are responsible for spreading AIDS infections. Recently I saw the Minister of Health, Dr Aaron Motsoaledi, on TV. He said, this issue about blessers is disgusting and nauseating! So look after yourself, Roli.'

'Thanks for the explanation, ma'am.'

* * *

'What did Ma'am Legodi say?' Khomisa asked Rolivhuwa.

Rolivhuwa told Khomisa what Ms Legodi told her.

'I told you that I suspected that there was something improper or impure, Roli. And you must be aware of one thing: According to the Bible bad company corrupts.'

'Ma'am Legodi said the same thing, Khomi.'

* * *

'I've realised that you are moving about with the company of the SCM members,' said Kedibone, 'because we sinners are stinking.'

'Who said that?' asked Rolivhuwa.

'The way you are behaving towards us. On Tuesday I saw you with Khomi. I saw her pointing towards us. What was she saying?'

'She was saying people who aren't born-again Christians are good at certain things.'

'Certain things like what? Getting drunk and ...?'

Rolivhuwa interrupted her with loud laughter. 'Ach, don't be negative, Kedi!'

'I was just wondering if she could say anything good about us.'

'I'm learning a few good things about Khomi's company, call them a crazy bunch. They even speak good English because they read the Bible.'

Kedibone frowned. 'Meneer Majola speaks good English, and he says it's because he is reading Zakes Mda and Es'kia Mphahlele's novels.'

Rolivhuwa shrugged.

* * *

Rolivhuwa felt bad when Kedibone said she was avoiding them because they were bad girls. So to prove that it was not the case Rolivhuwa began to spend more time with them than with Khomisa and the other Christians.

Kedibone was good at mathematics while Rolivhuwa was good at accounting. The two also visited each other during weekends to learn from each other. One weekend while Kedibone was visiting Rolivhuwa, her mother (Rolivhuwa's), who had a medical history of epilepsy, collapsed and they called an ambulance. When the ambulance was delayed, Kedibone phoned the man she referred to as her boyfriend. Minutes later a silver-grey BMW arrived and out of the car walked a pot-bellied, well-dressed, bald man in his mid-forties, displaying sunglasses on his head. Rolivhuwa knew immediately that he was Kedibone's sugar daddy.

'Bra Guff,' Kedibone addressed the man, 'Roli is my friend, so please do your best to help.'

Guff never disappointed; he sent Rolivhuwa's mother to a private hospital where she received the best treatment.

As a result, Rolivhuwa became indebted to Kedibone.

The following weekend Guff took Rolivhuwa and Kedibone to a shopping mall where they watched a movie. He gave them money for tickets, food and other expenses. Late in the afternoon he sent his driver to collect them and to take them to their homes.

The friendship between Rolivhuwa and Kedibone thrived and the following weekend Kedibone invited her to her home; there Kedibone sent Guff an SMS, asking him to send two fried chicken take-away packets, chips and fruit juices which were delivered within an hour. Kedibone gave Rolivhuwa a copy of a women's magazine. Rolivhuwa read a story about how some celebrities boasted about their relationships with sugar daddies. Kedibone handed Rolivhuwa taxi fare to get home.

3

At school Rolivhuwa and Kedibone were like hand in glove, always inseparable. They shared food and continued to visit each other. Days became weeks, and weeks gave birth to months and it was soon June. They wrote the half-year tests. During the final week when the learners had nothing to do except to add the number of days for the purpose of their school reports, Khomisa cornered Rolivhuwa and invited her to attend a Christian youth rally.

'It's an event you must not miss. There'll be lots of gospel music, and wonderful motivational speakers,' Khomisa smiled at Rolivhuwa, 'Roli, I'll give you a ticket,' promised Khomisa, 'please don't say "No," Roli!'

'No, I'm not interested, Khomi.'

Rolivhuwa walked away while Khomisa stood open-mouthed.

* * *

It was the last day at school and the learners wore home clothes. They were milling about the school yard, waiting to go home at 10am. Kedibone sat with Rolivhuwa in the sports field.

'Tomorrow, on Saturday, Bra Guff wants to throw a little party for us,' said Kedibone. 'So you are invited.'

'Thank you *chomi ya ka*. What's the venue?'

'Guess where? Monte Casino.'

'That's cool!'

'Bra Guff has asked his friend to join us. You see you must meet new people other than Guff and me. Fun is nicer if there are more people.'

'Thanks, Kedi.'

'So tell your parents that you are attending my birthday party and that you'll sleep at my place.'

Rolivhuwa nodded with a smile.

* * *

It was 5pm on Saturday. Rolivhuwa's mother was thrilled to see a silver-grey BMW waiting for her daughter at the gate. She felt proud that her next-door neighbours would see that an expensive car parked at her house. Rolivhuwa lied and said that Guff was Kedibone's uncle.

When they arrived in the foyer of the Monte Casino five-star hotel, Rolivhuwa saw a slightly overweight man smiling at them.

'Bigvy Masemola,' the man introduced himself.

'Roli Ramabulana,' said Rolivhuwa softly.

'I've seen your face, babe,' said Bigvy.

'Really?'

'Yes. You came to buy atchar at my café.'

'I'm pleased that *ntate* Masemola knows me.'

'You can call me bra Bigvy.'

Rolivhuwa smiled broadly, and she was able to relax. They went to sit on the couch where they were served with drinks. She saw Kedibone sipping a glass of wine.

Kedibone flashed a smile towards Rolivhuwa. 'You can taste it *chomi ya ka*. Wine cheers people up. You need to relieve the exam stress and forget about Solomon Mahlangu High for a moment.'

Rolivhuwa chuckled and Bigvy's face brightened.

'You can add just a little to your grape juice,' Kedibone coaxed. 'Wine will also give you an appetite.'

Raising a half glass of wine Rolivhuwa grinned towards Bigvy who touched her glass with his.

'Bless you!' said Bigvy who looked on with a huge smile as Rolivhuwa sipped the wine hesitantly.

The wine was at first a little bitter for Rolivhuwa, but as she sipped more she began to enjoy it and she soon asked for another glass. She asked for something salty and she snacked on salted fried snoek fish. Her inhibitions were totally broken and she spoke freely and loudly. Kedibone asked to go to the bathroom and soon Guff joined her and they were nowhere to be seen. Bigvy inquired about Rolivhuwa's family and she told him about her brother who was unemployed and often lived with his friends.

'I can see that you come from a struggling family, and I want help where I can, if I'm welcome to play a role,' said Bigvy.

'I'll appreciate any help, bra Bigvy.'

'So what do you want to be?'

'An accountant.'

'That's no small dream for a girl from a low-income family. So you need someone who will help you to achieve it; someone you can lean on, and I happen to be that kind of a person.'

She blushed unexpectedly, perhaps owing to a feeling that Bigvy's gesture was too good and too soon to be true.

Her blush turned into a grin and matured into a shy smile. 'Thank you, bra Bigvy.'

'Allow me to take care of you, babe, and I can make life easy for you, so that you can realise your dream. Bless you!'

'Thank you, bra Bigvy.'

Bigvy grinned. 'What do you do if you want a lovely dress, an expensive cellphone, a laptop and pocket money, but you can't afford them?'

Rolivhuwa smiled shyly. 'I don't know, bra Bigvy.'

'It's simple. Find a blesser.'

Rolivhuwa broke into giggles.

'Yes, a blesser. And ...' he pointed to his chest, 'Bigvy is your blessing on two legs.'

He chuckled and she emulated him.

'Thank you, bra Bigvy.'

He brushed her hand. 'Listen babe, if you play your part I'll play mine, big-time! You know what I mean?'

She knew what he meant and she gave a coquettish smile and he responded by brushing her thigh. She held his naughty hand, but her weak grip made him feel she wouldn't mind to be taken to a place where they could make love. He grabbed her hand and began to scratch her palm. She was tickled and she laughed. He salivated when he saw her tongue, and he felt like embracing and kissing her.

An hour later they had had dinner and they went to a disco. Bigvy was afforded an opportunity to touch Rolivhuwa. Her tight-fitting pitch-black silken dress accentuated her breasts and bottoms. He salivated as if he were a cannibal. When a slow-paced song was playing, he began feeling her breasts and exploring her waist and the top part of her buttocks. He looked deep into her eyes; she could not blink because she was drunk. But when he rubbed her buttocks she removed his hands.

They went to the bar where they had beers, whiskey and wine. Because she had been dancing, she was thirsty for wine; she asked for it and Bigvy made it available. As she drank, Kedibone was delighted that Rolivhuwa was enjoying the wine. Guff winked at Bigvy who winked back. The men took their sugar babies and walked with them to their rooms.

4

When Rolivhuwa woke up the next morning she was shocked to see herself naked, lying next to a snoring man. She looked at him closely; his mouth hung open and he looked awfully unattractive. A needle could be lost in his hairy chest, and his big stomach utterly disgusted her.

She looked for any sign of a used condom and she found none. She sobered up to realise that she might be infected with an STI or even HIV. She felt that she had foul breath. A terrible headache worsened the situation. She began to ask herself many questions: *Do all sugar babies pay such a huge price? Is the life of a sugar baby such a sacrifice? Am I going to live the life of a prostitute? Can I change my mind at this stage and get out of the relationship? Or is it too late to opt out?* She decided that she would wiggle herself out of the relationship. But another thought whispered, *No, please just wait!*

When Bigvy ultimately awoke he gave her a smile from ear to ear, but he soon realised that she wasn't in a jovial mood. She wasn't making eye contact with him. He tickled her face but she would not respond with a chuckle or laughter.

'Com'on Roli, cheer up!'

'I'm okay, bra Bigvy, I just happen to have a terrible headache.'

'A headache isn't a train-smash, baby.'

He put on his clothes and walked to his men's mini handbag, opened it and handed her a headache powder.

'Roli, I appreciate that our relationship is new,' said Bigvy, 'and it can as a result be painful like a new pair of shoes. As time goes on you'll get used to it and have a lot of fun.'

She forced a tired smile. They bathed, put on fresh clothes and went to the lobby for breakfast. Guff and Kedibone were already helping themselves to bacon and eggs. Rolivhuwa and Bigvy joined their table and enjoyed their breakfast.

Bigvy was delighted to see Rolivhuwa wearing the smile he had seen the previous day. They took their time, spending nearly two hours in the dining hall. Guff asked Kedibone if they would like to watch a movie, and she said she was interested. As they rose to their feet, Kedibone asked Rolivhuwa to accompany her to the bathroom.

As they were on the way to the bathroom, Kedibone grabbed Rolivhuwa by her hand, 'Come, let's sit over there. I want to have a girl-to-girl talk with you.'

Kedibone smoothed her Peruvian weave towards the nape of her neck. 'If your man is fifty and you are whatever age, what's their problem? Age is just a number!'

'Ya, *chomi ya ka.*'

'And you must stay away from girls like Khomi. She'll be saying: "*hee-hee* sex is sinful." And if you can read the Bible carefully you'll discover that there were many sugar daddies.'

'Is that so?'

'Yes! The great man Abraham was a blesser of a black girl called Hagar.'

Rolivhuwa reacted with puzzlement.

'To give a local example,' Kedibone continued, 'Nelson Mandela has been Graça Machel's sugar daddy. Not financially speaking, but in terms of their age differences.'

Rolivhuwa chuckled. 'How do you know? Is that mentioned in his *Long Walk to Freedom*?'

'No, you won't find that in the book. Remember that he met Graça after divorcing Winnie. But I can't say that Graça was Mandela's sugar baby because he met her when she was over fifty years old. But because of the wide age gap, he's still her sugar daddy.'

Kedibone's cellphone beeped and she attended to it. 'Let me turn it to silent.' She paused for a moment as she dropped the cellphone into her handbag. 'Okay let's talk about ourselves.

'I can assure you *chomi ya ka,*' Kedibone continued,

'you've hit the jackpot.' Kedibone opened her palms. They smacked each other's palms and high-fived. 'Just give him what he wants and you'll get what you want. Don't be apologetic. Just behave confidently like Khanyi. I know that people will be talking, *pjerr-pjerr-pjerr*! Let them talk; if you live in poverty what are they doing for you?'

'Nothing,' responded Rolivhuwa.

'They are just reacting from nothing but jealousy.'

'It's true *chomi ya ka*!'

Kedibone grinned and winked, sticking out her tongue. 'So how was your first experience ... you know what I mean, with bra Bigvy?'

Rolivhuwa blushed.

Kedibone brushed Rolivhuwa's arm. 'Com'n, don't be shy.'

Rolivhuwa giggled. 'It was okay, Kedi.'

'Just okay?'

Rolivhuwa grinned and shrugged. 'What about you, Kedi?'

'I had a great time. Let me share some advice with you. When you are in love with a sugar daddy, you learn a lot. You soon learn to be adventurous. These old guys come for us because they are bored by their wives. A woman just opens her thighs, looks up to the ceiling and waits until it is over. And she talks a lot about debts and the children. And they also don't change the positions. They haven't heard of a doggy or woman-on-top styles.

'So, be adventurous and add spice to your sex life. You see, us young ones should give them value for their money. Sex must be fun, baby. Massage his chest, kiss his nipples, make those seductive "woo-woo" sounds and when he's coming scratch his balls.'

Rolivhuwa chortled and pinched Kedibone's arm.

'Yes,' Kedibone continued. 'If you want to get the best from him, be romantic Roli. As I said, variety is the spice of life. Make life more interesting by bathing together. Wash and touch each other to heighten the mood and later have it in the shower.'

Rolivhuwa giggled. 'In the shower?'

'Yes. In the shower. Or on the floor. No squeaky bedsprings. You can also have it on the couch, in the swimming pool or in the car. Sometimes get on top of him and let him know you are in charge. The possibilities are endless, *chomi ya ka*.'

They smacked each other's palms, high-fived and laughed aloud.

* * *

After the movie they returned to have drinks at the bar. It was noon. At 1pm they had lunch. Guff winked at Bigvy, and the two sugar daddies took their sugar babies to their rooms.

'Roli, I told you that I'm the one who can help you realise your dream,' said Bigvy, as they sat on the bed.

'Talk is cheap, but to demonstrate to you that I mean business, here is a little gift.'

He handed her a brand-new cellphone.

'Oh thank you so much, bra Big,' said Rolivhuwa, who pecked him on his dry lips with her lips.

'And for your pocket money, here is something for you,' he opened his bulging purse and took out a stack of banknotes. 'You can count the money.'

She counted the banknotes. 'It's R2 000, bra Big.'

'It's all yours, baby. Bless you!'

'Thank you very much, bra Big.'

Bigvy stood up and began to unbutton his shirt.

He grinned. 'Now let's have one for the road, baby.'

She began to undress.

'When my eyes landed on you, as you came to my café for the first time,' said Bigvy, as they got into bed, 'I thought: *If only I could get between those fresh shining thighs ...!*'

She responded with a faint smile.

'I could be 50 years old and you may be twenty. What's the problem? Age is just a number. I don't understand why people should be concerned when some of us have an appetite for sugar babies. You hear people saying: "*Hee-hee* sugar daddies are corrupting our girls!" There's a minister who always says a lot of ugly things about us.'

'Who? The Minister of Health?'

'Yes, Dr Motsoaledi. What's his problem? Are we not entitled to exercise our rights and choices as consumers?

'At a restaurant, someone will ask for beef from a full-grown cow or a one-day-old calf. If you want to have a car you can choose to drive a sleek Mercedes, a Ford Fiesta, or a Mini Cooper. So what is the problem if I choose fresh thighs and a tight vagina? In Afrikaans they say, "*Die ou bok hou van jong blare.*" – The old goat is fond of tender leaves.'

He brushed her thighs and other parts of her body, and they cuddled and exchanged kisses. She had declined to drink wine; so she was now sober. As they made love, she realised for the first time that he looked like an ugly toad. She felt his heavy weight, and his rough penetration made her feel like screaming, '*Joo-mma-wee!*' She heard him shouting, '*Bless you!* Dr Motsoaledi or not!' as he climaxed. She was honest with herself – she hated how he smelt, and what he was doing to her.

At that moment she had two hearts: The first heart said, 'Roli, get out this relationship.' But the second one whispered, 'Please wait, perhaps you'll get used to the new shoes.'

5

When Rolivhuwa's mother asked her how the outing was, she replied that it was great. She showed her mother the cellphone and money and lied that she had been given them by her friend's rich father. Her mother received the gifts appreciatively: *May God bless that big-hearted man!*

The following day in the evening after they had had supper, while Rolivhuwa was washing the dishes, she said to her mother: 'Mama, I can't go on lying to you, the cellphone and the money come from a certain man ... he's an older guy. He promised me that he is prepared to help me realise my dream.'

'Who is that man, Vhovho? And where does he come from?' asked her mother. 'I must know that man, Vhovho. If he's getting money by selling drugs, then please return the cellphone and the money.'

'He lives in Mamelodi and he's a businessman.'

Her mother kept quiet for a long moment.

'If the man loves you, and you love him, what can I say?' Her mother shrugged her shoulders. 'As long as he doesn't disturb you in your studies.'

'He won't disturb me, Mama. In fact he wants to see to it that I should do well in my studies.'

'May God bless that big-hearted man!'

* * *

On a Saturday morning, Bigvy's red BMW cruised to a halt in front of Rolivhuwa's yard and hooted. Rolivhuwa, who was ready and was elegantly dressed in smart casuals, rushed out of the house.

'Mama, I'll introduce the man when we come back.'

Her mother looked on as the BMW drove away, very pleased that some of her next-door neighbours had seen the expensive car that had come to collect her daughter.

* * *

Three hours later the red BMW parked in front of Rolivhuwa's gate. Her mother was standing in the doorway facing the gate, holding a feather-duster, a cloth and furniture polish. Bigvy and Rolivhuwa entered the yard groaning under the weight of several plastic shopping bags. Her mother hurried to relieve them of the load.

'Mama, meet Mr Bigvy Masemola,' said Rolivhuwa. 'Bra Bigvy, my mother.'

Bigvy and her mother greeted each other by shaking hands.

'As I told you, Mama, he is the man who is prepared to help me realise my dream.'

'I'm pleased to meet him, my child,' said her mother, 'what shall this big man eat? Can I prepare tea for him?'

'No *mamazala*, don't worry, I'm in hurry,' said Bigvy.

Her mother was amazed to hear Bigvy, who looked older than her, addressing her as *mamazala*.

* * *

The following week, Bigvy sent a draughtsman to Rolivhuwa's home. Within a week, when the house plan had been approved, their three-roomed house was increased by two more rooms. Three days later her mother and the next-door neighbours saw a red BMW, followed by a furniture truck, approaching their house. Rolivhuwa was with Bigvy.

'Mama, we decided to give you the surprise of your life,' said Rolivhuwa elatedly. 'When I told bra Bigvy it was your birthday he said, you surely deserve this little gift.'

Rolivhuwa's mother hugged and kissed her daughter and also bear-hugged Bigvy.

The furniture people offloaded a seven-piece dining room suite, a five-piece Italian-styled lounge suite and a hi-fi set with huge speakers. Her mother kneeled, applauded twice, looking at Bigvy.

'Mr Masemola, I don't know how to thank you for all that you've done,' said Rolivhuwa's mother, 'God has really wiped off my tears. Thank you very very much, Mr Masemola.' She applauded twice as she looked heavenward. 'May God bless this big-hearted man!'

'You are welcome, *mamazala*,' said Bigvy. 'If I'm able to help someone, why can't I do that?'

* * *

When the next-door neighbours and relatives commented on how blessed her daughter was to have a rich boyfriend, her mother said: 'Well, what I can say? God doesn't give directly with His hand; He uses other people.'

During the rest of the holidays Bigvy flaunted Rolivhuwa to his friends, and went with her to many hotels, and places of entertainment around Mamelodi, such as Boy Mafa, Jack Buda, Mississippi and others.

* * *

During the first week after school had reopened, curious learners noticed that a red BMW came to collect Rolivhuwa. Many students and learners thought that Bigvy was Rolivhuwa's uncle. Kedibone told her friends that she was the match-maker of Bigvy and Rolivhuwa, and the hot news was lapped up by the gossip-mongers among the learners. During break, Rolivhuwa ate chicken and rice and drank high-quality fruit juice. She had parted company with dust-covered *sphatlo* and the putrid smell of low-quality juices. She was seen answering her expensive cellphone and laughing aloud.

On the Friday of the same week after school, Rolivhuwa and Kedibone waited at the gate where their sugar daddies often picked them up. A group of girls stood beside them, their eyes burning with envy and curiosity.

'What's your problem with boy students?' asked one of the girls. 'You don't like them because they have no money?'

'I'll give you three reasons why falling in love with a student doesn't work for me,' responded Kedibone. 'First, they are immature, second, they are always broke and third, they are sexually inexperienced; there's just quantity not quality. They just do bang-bang, and boast that they had five rounds. A sugar daddy takes his time; he may give you one round per night, but that's unforgettable!' At this point she put her hands on her head. 'Ooh, I don't know how to explain it!'

The girls guffawed, applauded and even wiggled their hips.

Rolivhuwa told them the good things that Bigvy had done for her and for her family.

'My man is spending more than R1 000 per month for Estée Lauder cosmetics and perfumes,' Rolivhuwa boasted, 'this includes manicures and pedicures. When he took me to the hotel for the first time he gave me a French perfume,' at this point she pursed her lips and rolled her eyes 'called *La Petite Robe noʼne.*'

Some of the girls oohed and aahed while others chortled.

'*Hamba wena*!' exclaimed one of the girls.

'He doesn't buy me cheap clothes from Pep. No. I make sure he buys famous brands such as Gucci, Jean Paul Gaultier and other top brands. I also get R500 airtime a week,' Rolivhuwa continued, 'This weekend he's paying for the unveiling of my grandmother's tomb stone. And a week after next, he's sponsoring my birthday party.'

What she could not tell them, however, was that Bigvy had commanded her to lengthen her skirt so that she should not tempt the teachers and boys at school.

Guff came to collect Kedibone and the girls left one by one to catch their transport, until Rolivhuwa found herself facing Khomisa, who had been quietly listening to Kedibone and Rolivhuwa boasting about their sugar daddies.

Khomisa smiled at Rolivhuwa. 'So you've decided to be someone's sugar baby?'

'I can see that you are ready with a Bible verse, *mamfundisi*! With your sermon: "Hee hee sex is sinful, wala-wala-wala ..."'

'Okay, let me speak about common morals. Being paid for sex is nothing but a white-washed form of prostitution. Period!'

'You can call it whatever you want. As long as I can sleep well at night, I'm not bothered. And I have no respect ... In fact I don't care about people who are too quick to moralise but cannot put a plate of food on my table!'

'Listen, Roli, I have a verse for you. Life and death are right in your hands. So today please choose life.'

'I've chosen a sweet life instead of a miserable life.'

'Let me be frank with you, Roli.'

'I know what you are going to say.'

'I have something different today.'

Rolivhuwa shrugged.

'You know what?' said Khomisa, 'You've swallowed the devil's bait.'

'I knew you would say that'.

'Listen, Roli. You are busy drinking poison sweetened by honey! When a sugar daddy spoils you with money and material things, it's honey.'

'And how does that poison come into this?'

'I'm getting to that. When life seems to be all honey, you ignore the poison, but the time soon comes when the poison will sting, you'll have to face the truth.'

'I suspected you would speak like this because you are jealous of me.' At that moment Rolivhuwa took a step back.

'The Bible says ...,' started Khomisa.

Rolivhuwa fidgeted and began to turn away. 'No, I don't want to listen to your Bible nonsense! Sis, you are jealous of me because I am blessed!' she scowled.

'The Bible says,' Khomisa shouted, waving a finger at her, '"You shall reap what you sow!"'

Rolivhuwa walked away blocking her ears with her index fingers. 'Listen, I'm blessed and proud of it!' she hollered.

6

In the middle of a new week after the unveiling of her grandmother's tombstone, Rolivhuwa handed out beautifully designed invitation cards for her birthday party to a few students; it was planned for Sunday. On that Friday during break, she was surrounded by several girls, including Kedibone, when her cellphone rang. They held their breath as she pulled her black iPhone 4s 16GB out of her mini-handbag.

After answering the call she beamed a smile towards the girls. 'Guess what, girls; the celebrity Khanyi Mbalula will be attending *my* birthday parddy!'

'Ooh! Ooh!' the girls shouted and cheered.

* * *

On Saturday, late in the afternoon, Bigvy saw to it that a blue-and-white tent was pitched and that chairs were supplied. On Sunday morning an elaborate sound system was in place. An hour before the party was to start at noon, her friends and chosen classmates were lounging inside and around the tent, eating snacks and holding glasses filled with wine or cold drinks. Rolivhuwa was preparing herself. Kedibone was sitting in the tent next to her sugar daddy, Guff. Kedibone's classmates kept pointing to Guff. Rolivhuwa's relatives, her uncle, two aunts and her mother's sisters, were sitting in the house.

A few minutes before the party started, when Bigvy arrived, he was delighted to find Rolivhuwa immaculately dressed for the party: she had had her hair done to match the style worn by Lira. She wore Magic slim-leg jeans, a grey pin-stripe jacket, a sky-blue cotton round-neck tank that exposed a little of the top part of her breasts and deep purple nail polish on her fingers and toes. She told Kedibone that her blue-and-white platform heel shoes were by a famous Italian designer called Gino Paoli. She had rolled up the sleeves of the jacket, to expose an expensive Victorinox Swiss wrist-watch on her left arm.

In a warm-up session those who could not resist the jivy music displayed their footwork. Kedibone, the programme director, stood on the right of Rolivhuwa who was sitting next to Bigvy. Kedibone proposed a toast and all sipped an imported Champagne in a toast to Rolivhuwa's health. Bigvy stood up, smiled and handed Rolivhuwa a red heart-shaped card.

'Roli, please read what's written at the back of the card,' said Bigvy.

'Blessed and proud of it!' Rolivhuwa read aloud.

As applause subsided, he handed her two gift-wrapped boxes and she kissed him as she received them.

'I want her to open the first gift,' said Bigvy, 'so that you can all see how much I love her!'

'It's a laptop!' Rolivhuwa proudly announced after taking her time to open the present.

All applauded uproariously.

'Yes, it's an Apple Mac!' said Bigvy. 'Why this gift? Because I want to see her realising her dream!'

Again the people applauded.

'Bless you!' said Bigvy.

They exchanged kisses.

'Now the second gift,' said Bigvy.

Rolivhuwa tore open the wrapping. 'It's a ...' she paused to read the label. 'Louis Vuitton handbag!'

Bigvy and Rolivhuwa again exchanged kisses.

Lunch was provided by a catering company whose waiters and waitresses wore black and white. Soon liquor was served and the imbibers began to raise their voices.

An older aunt said to Rolivhuwa: 'Child of my sister, when the sun shines for you,' she said as she sipped wine, 'bask in it.'

Her uncle's wife nodded. But the younger aunt revealed her scepticism when she said: 'You'll pardon me my people. I don't know why I have a feeling that this relationship is going to turn sour.'

'Why must you think of such a bad thing?' the elder aunt disagreed. 'Aren't you happy that we also have a blessee? And how do you know if this relationship is going to end in marriage?'

'Blessers don't think of marriage. Anyway, this man's wife is still alive.'

'Well, rich people can marry more than one wife; so he can marry her according to African customs, just like President Zuma,' said the aunt.

All the relatives had a good laugh.

'If her man can throw such a big party for her when she is only 18,' said her elder aunt, 'what should we expect when she turns 21? I'm certain celebrities and even sons and daughters of top businessmen and cabinet ministers could be invited.'

'My people, I don't agree with you. As adults you should be guiding the child, and not be her cheerleaders. To be honest you are selfish,' the younger aunt said.

'What do you mean, Bertha?'

'We'll talk some day. I don't want to make a scene in front of Roli's blesser and her schoolmates.'

Rolivhuwa walked hand-in-hand with Bigvy to chat to groups of friends. 'Are you all right guys?' she inquired.

'Oh yes!' was the response. Some of them responded by raising their thumbs.

Kedibone walked over to Rolivhuwa and said: '*Chomi ya ka*, some of the girls want to know where Khanyi is.'

'Some of you might have read in the Sunday newspapers,' said Bigvy, 'that Khanyi has crashed her BMW into the wall of their expensive house in Sandton, following a quarrel with her husband, Mandla.'

There were sounds of *Mh, mh. Mh. Ag-shem* and some clicks of pity.

'But please let this not raise eyebrows, because lovers quarrel at times don't they?'

'Yes!' chorused the voices.

The party continued, more liquor came, the revellers drank, and music was food for the ear.

Bigvy, still holding Rolivhuwa's hand, walked and sat at the table of relatives.

'*Mamazala*,' he addressed her mother, 'When she goes to the technikon next year, I'm going to buy her a *smallernyana* smart car.'

'Thank you, Mr Masemola,' said her mother who turned towards her people and said: 'Well, what I can say, my people? God doesn't give directly with His hand; He uses other people.'

7

For weeks Rolivhuwa's friends and schoolmates talked about her birthday party. Responding to the relatives and next-door neighbours' positive comments, her mother said: 'Well, what I can say? God doesn't give directly with His hand; He uses other people.'

The flip side of her much envied public life was something Rolivhuma would dare not share with Kedibone or her mother. The honeymoon period was over, and she had to face hard life. She had to make a hard choice or live a lie for many months to come. The generous Bigvy applied the philosophy of: 'The hand that gives must receive. If I spoil you, you must spoil me!' So the more he gave to Rolivhuwa, the more sex he expected, and that was what he got. Rumour had it that he was using an indigenous Viagra called *sekanama*, and that his late father was a herbalist in Ga-Sekhukhune in Limpopo. Another rumour was that Bigvy had boasted among his friends that he was keeping his sugar baby awake all night, making love.

The question that never gave her peace was: *How are my mother and Kedibone going to react when they hear the real truth, that I'm getting tired of being his* sex object? That while I care about his money, I hate to see him lying on top of me, sweating as he pumps up and down, sometimes farting as he reached his climax, shouting, 'Bless you!'?

Rolivhuwa heard from older women who had been students or workers in Europe and England that there was a kind of sugar daddy who showered their sugar babes with money and presents without expecting sex. *I wish I could live in that part of the world*, she often mused.

Although Bigvy was gentle during love-making most of the time, at times he was so rough that he left her vagina bruised and she would take a few days before she healed, and before she healed completely he demanded more sex. And whenever she pleaded: *Not tonight, bra Bigvy*, he accused her of being unfaithful. She was compelled to tell him what she said was nothing but the truth. *No, it can't be mine. It must be the young, fast and full-blooded penises that have wreaked the havoc you are telling me about*. That how he often responded.

His reaction left her very frustrated. This source of conflict was to both of them so sensitive that they found it difficult to share with any other person. That deep-seated secret began to build a thin wall between her and Kedibone; she would at times become absent-minded while talking to her bosom-friend. As a result, Kedibone often asked her: Are you still with me?

The problem remained unresolved as Bigvy continued to take her out to restaurants and hotels.

She would enjoy her meal during the day but she knew that at night conflict would flare out. That created tension, and to solve the problem he would ply her with a lot of gifts and money. She once said to herself, 'I don't think I'll ever get used to the new shoes. They continue to be painful. At one time during an argument he punched her in her face; she went home with a black eye; she would not breathe a word about the fact that Bigvy demanded more sex while she did not feel like having it because of her vaginal injury. She lied to her mother that she had knocked her eye on a chair at the hotel.

While the black eye was healing and he had taken her to a medical practitioner who was his friend, she refused to go to school. He bought her expensive brown-tinted sunglasses, but her educators would not allow a learner to wear sunglasses during class time. So she lied to anyone who asked a direct question that her jealous ex-boyfriend had inflicted the black eye and that she had laid a charge of assault with the police.

Bigvy was fond of taking her to hotels on Friday evenings. He would drop her at her mother's gate on Saturday morning. If she had no tests to prepare for the following week he would insist that they should spend another night at the hotel. At times he would ask her to bring books to the hotel, and he would assure her that he would give her time to read during the day while he went to attend to his business or to share a slice of his time with his miserable wife. Three of his five children were older than Rolivhuwa, and he was proud of that. In order to assure Rolivhuwa of his undying and faithful love he began to share with her the marital problem he was experiencing because of their relationship.

'My wife is aware of our relationship,' he said to her, 'and do you know what she said just before I came to visit you?'

'Tell me,' said Rolivhuwa.

'She said: "I'm going to mutilate the vagina of that bitch!"'

'So what are you telling me, bra Bigvy? That my life is in danger because of your unhappy bitter wife?'

'This impending danger is in fact making me more determined to have you than to give up,' he said.

'I think you should go back to your wife and children.'

'You tell me to go back to my wife and children? Aren't you happy that you have me? Mh? I can see what's happening here: I have built your mother's house and furnished it, I've given you money, an expensive cellphone, sponsored your grandmother's tombstone and splashed out on a great birthday party. Now that you have what you wanted you want to throw me away like a banana peel because you want young blood.' He breathed heavily, his eyes blood-shot and burning with anger. He beat his palm with his fist. 'My girl you aren't going to leave me!'

Rolivhuwa shook her head. 'No, bra Big, you've got it all wrong. If your wife was not threatening me with violence it would be better. I don't want to be killed by hitmen hired by your bitter wife.'

'No, that's not going to happen, Roli.'

'How can you be sure?'

He grinned. 'I'll hire bodyguards for you.'

'*Ntate* Masemola, I had no idea that I would live this kind of a life. No one has prepared me.'

He was sorely disappointed that she was addressing him as *Ntate* Masemola, and not *bra* Bigvy or better still, *bra Big*. He felt as if she was pushing him away from her.

'You know what, Roli, if you want good things in life you must be prepared to take a risk.'

'Yes, but that doesn't mean I should be careless. If I see danger coming I should avoid it. It would be foolish of me to …'

'You have a convenient excuse, eh? My girl, you aren't going to leave me!'

She buried her face in her palms and began to sob. He moved closer to her and squeezed her shoulders.

PART TWO

8

One Friday afternoon Rolivhuwa's mother was busy ironing when she heard her daughter sobbing in her room. She entered Rolivhuwa's room and inquired what the problem was.

'I've serious problems with Mr Masemola,' she looked at her mother with tearful eyes. 'Mama, I have made a big blunder.'

She pulled up a chair, sat on it and folded her arms. 'What are you telling me, my child?'

'I've made a huge mistake by falling for a sugar daddy.'

'You haven't made any mistake. No. Say, you are encountering a problem. My girl, you've got to learn to ignore the problem and count your blessings. Aren't you happy that you are making a good life for all of us?'

'At what price? I can't go on pleasing you and my friends, at my expense.'

'I still don't understand, my child.'

'You know what's happening, Mama. You know that I'm in love ... why should I call it love? You know that I'm sleeping with Mr Masemola ... he's calling you *mamazala*, as if he has paid you lobola. Mama, I've stopped ...'

'Mr Masemola could pay lobola if you become sensible.'

'Am I not making sense that you are turning a blind eye to the fact that I'm sleeping with Mr Masemola for money? I've stopped being a girl and have turned into a prostitute, with your blessing! Mama, I'm convinced that you don't really love me!'

'I love you, my girl.'

'You are lying to yourself. You know that you love money and material blessings more than you care for me. I can't go on being a whore with your approval. So I have decided that bra Bigvy isn't going to touch me as from today.'

Her mother took a deep breath before she looked at her feet in thought. She grinned as she maintained eye contact with Rolivhuwa. 'Have you told Mr Masemola that you don't want him to touch you?'

'Yes, and he insisted that I can't leave him.'

'I agree with him. My girl, lovers must have quarrels because we are not yet in heaven. So my advice as your mother who saw many, many troubles is: *Persevere my child*. You'll ...'

'Mama, I feel I've had enough and I don't think ...'

'Listen! You'll arrive at the top of the hill and life will be better thereafter until you ascend another hill again. I became widowed when your brother was six years old and you were two. What did I do? I didn't put my hands on the heads and say: "Life is too heavy, I'm giving up!"'

'*Aiwa*! I used to leave your brother in the care of your grandmother, while I carried you behind my back going to work for a white woman in the city, as a domestic. Today you are eighteen years old and God had blessed you with such a sweet, generous man like Mr Masemola. When you introduced him to me, what did you say? You said: "Mama, meet Mr Bigvy Masemola; he is the man who is prepared to help me realise my dream." Didn't you say that?'

'Yes, Mama, but the circumstances have ...'

'Listen, let me finish! You haven't started with your dream and now you are thinking of quitting. You'll be foolish to walk out of the relationship. What you must remember is that there are thousands of girls your age who are waiting with open hands saying: "Throw away so that we should receive!"'

'Let them take him, and they'll soon get tired of being sex machines.'

'Vhovho, I'm your mother, and you're going to obey my advice: Don't give up. If you give up, you'll regret it, and it'll be too late for tears! Your grandfather was fond of a Tshivenda idiom that says: "He who makes me walk at night-time, I shall thank him in the morning." You will have tears on your cheeks, but you'll smile with tears still on your cheeks and say: "Mama, I'm glad I've heeded your advice."'

* * *

During the new week Rolivhuwa stayed away from the company of other girls, including Kedibone. During breaks she only walked to the toilets and returned to her classroom. On the third day during break Kedibone found Rolivhuwa standing in the company of her classmates and beckoned her over. They went to speak in a secluded place behind the girls' toilets.

'Roli, why are you keeping to yourself?' she demanded.

'No there's nothing wrong, *chomi ya ka*. I don't have enough time for my studies because, during weekends, bra Bigvy takes my time.'

'We are missing your company. And I'm concerned because everybody says your usual smile has disappeared. If there's any problem please tell me. I'll talk to Guff and he'll take it up with bra Bigvy.'

'No there's nothing wrong, *chomi ya ka*.'

'There's nothing seriously wrong if lovers quarrel. You know *chomi ya ka*, I've realised that love tastes sweeter after a quarrel.'

Rolivhuwa tried to release a chuckle but she failed dismally.

'Let me give you a piece of advice,' said Kedibone. 'You can take it or leave it. I'm going to be honest. You are going to face many challenges. But you should be wise to count your blessings and not your problems. And let me share something juicy with you, *chomi ya ka*. Guff told me that he and Bigvy are planning to take us to Mauritius, the island of love!'

Rolivhuwa shook her head. 'No! I'm not interested. Listen, Kedi, let me not be unfair to myself.'

'Why are you saying that?'

Rolivhuwa kept quiet for a moment looking Kedibone straight into her eyes. 'I'm going to tell you nothing but the truth: The second day when we made love, I didn't really enjoy it *chomi ya ka*. The first day, to be honest, I was drunk, because *you* encouraged me to drink wine.'

'So I forced your mouth open and made you drink the wine?'

'You kept encouraging me until I ...'

Kedibone scowled. 'I guess you will soon stop calling me "*chomi ya ka*", if you are going in this direction. Continue!'

'Bra Bigvy was too heavy for me when we made love. And he looked like ...' Roliwhowa faltered, 'he looked like mh ... an ugly toad.'

'So I've opened your thighs and put an ugly toad on you breast? Well, have sex with a handsome guy and be poor!'

Rolivhuwa pointed a finger towards Kedibone. 'Don't talk nonsense, Kedi!'

'Shut up!'

'You shut up!'

9

Bigvy drove to Rolivhuwa's home in a jovial mood. He had drunk a good amount of *sekanama*, the indigenous Viagra, looking forward to having a terrific session of lovemaking. He hooted and waited as usual. Rolivhuwa's mother, who was in one of the bedrooms, saw him.

'Vhovho,' her mother hollered, 'Mr Masemola is waiting for you, please hurry up!'

'No, I can't go, Mama,' Rolivhuwa shouted from her bedroom, 'I'm very sick.'

Rolivhuwa quickly took a peeled onion and squeezed it into her eyes, which became instantly tearful. Her mother hurried to Rolivhuwa's bedroom, where she found her lying on the bed bending over, hugging her knees, groaning.

'No, Vhovho, you can't say you are sick. What's the problem?'

'Menstrual pains, Mama.'

'When did it start?'

Rolivhuwa grimaced. 'A few minutes ago.'

A knock could be heard at the door. 'Come in!' shouted Rolivhuwa's mother.

Rolivhuwa's mother walked out of her daughter's room, into the living room where Bigvy was waiting. 'Vhovho isn't well today, Mr Masemola,' she informed him after exchanging greetings with him. 'She's suffering from women's pains.'

'Is it so serious that she can't go out with me?'

'Sometimes her pains are so severe that she misses school.'

He gave her a quizzical look. '*Mamazala*, you are her mother, so I can't say you are lying.'

'Why would I lie, Mr Masemola? I'm disappointed that she's unable to go with you. You are so good to us, Mr Masemola.'

She was relieved that he was at peace. 'You can come and talk to her, if it's okay with you.'

'I don't want to enter the room. I'll speak to her from this room.'

He, however, knocked at the door of her bedroom.

'Please come in, bra Bigvy.'

He entered and stood near the door. He was elated to see her wearing the purple morning gown he had bought her.

'Roli my apple-tart, what kind of food do you want? I'll send one of my drivers to bring it.'

'No thanks, bra Big. I'm terribly sorry to disappoint you, bra Big,' said Rolivhuwa who maintained prolonged eye contact with Bigvy to ascertain from his eyes if her explanation was acceptable. 'I'm sure my mother told you what my problem is.'

'What is actually your problem?'

'It's what is called PMT – Premenstrual Tension. You are a man bra Big, you won't understand.'

'I'll understand if you will make me understand.'

'The nursing sister who visits our school and talks to the girls once a month says when PMT attacks a woman, she could have headaches, less sleep and even less sex desire, and other problems. You are a man bra Big, you won't …'

'It's all right, Roli. If you're unwell I shouldn't be unreasonable.'

'Thank you for being a gentleman, bra Big. As for food, please don't worry; I don't have appetite today. Perhaps tomorrow.'

He stepped closer to her bed and kissed her dry lips lightly. 'I'll see you tomorrow, Roli.'

'It's all right, bra Big.' She grinned as he stepped out of the room, delighted that her trick had been effective.

10

Bigvy was by habit a punctual person, in business and in his private life. He often boasted: *I'm black by colour but by keeping time I can shame a European.* So, in picking up Rolivhuwa he consistently observed time. She expected him to come to her home at 5pm that Saturday.

Rolivhuwa had to do chores such as washing, cleaning the house, cooking and studying. She had planned that by 4pm she would be done with everything. She would then sneak out of the house, pretending to go to the spaza shop.

She had thought it would be a good idea if she would go to the home of Tinini, a girl who had completed grade 12 from the same high school. She had not visited her for many months. Tinini's home was diagonally opposite Rolivhuwa's home. She hoped that from there she would be able to peep through the curtain to ascertain if Bigvy had come; she would perhaps ask Tinini to send her little sisters to look around for Bigvy and to monitor his movements.

Just as she was about to leave the house she saw Bigvy's BMW stopping at the gate. What could she do now? She had to think very fast. The first thought was to jump out the window and run to the back next-door neighbour's home; she was friendly with one of their daughters, and there was no fence to bother about. She heard the car hooting: *Pawpaw*!! Her heart began to beat fast.

She was anxious and she hated the picture of seeing herself sitting beside the man she felt must never touch her again. In a panic, she decided to run into her bedroom and hide in the wardrobe. She hid below a little heap of extra blankets and bed sheets that were used in winter. She breathed slowly.

'Vhovho!' her mother called. 'Mr Masemola is waiting at the gate! Please hurry up, and don't make him wait a second today!'

'Vhovho! Vhovho!' her mother called again, this time harshly.

She continued to breathe slowly, her heart thumping in her ears. She heard quick footsteps that stopped in the middle of the bedroom. 'Oh Jehovah! Where is she now?' said her mother, who sighed and smashed her palms together. 'Oh mysterious things never stop happening!'

'Koko!' It was Bigvy's voice.

'Come in Mr Masemola.' Rolivhuwa heard Bigvy's footsteps.

'You won't believe what I'm going to tell you, Mr Masemola,' said Rolivhuwa's mother after they had greeted each other.

'Is there any problem, *mamazala*?'

'Yes, a very serious problem, Mr Masemola,' she sighed. 'The girl has disappeared. She was in the house. She said she would go and buy something from the spaza and return home before you arrived. Now I don't know what happened to her. How can she just leave the house without telling me?' She brought her palms together again. 'Oh strange things never stop happening, Mr Masemola.'

'How far is the spaza?' asked Bigvy.

'It's a five-minute walk. Would you like to go and check there?'

'Let me wait. She's a responsible girl. I trust her.'

'Can I give you something to drink, Mr Masemola?'

'No thanks, *mamazala*.'

Minutes were like hours for Rolivhuwa. She uncovered her head as the winter blankets were too hot for her and it was too dark.

'I think I must go, *mamazala*, I must go!' said Bigvy, sounding impatient. 'If your daughter thinks I'm here to lick her arse, she has made a big mistake! Does she think Bigvy has a big heart for her *manga manga* business? Hee, this girl doesn't know Bigvy! She's playing with fire when there's water. My father was fond of saying you can beat a fool on the buttocks once but not twice! *Aowa*!

'Listen *mamazala*, tell your girl that Bigvy is no big fool, okay?' He jingled the car keys. 'I'm going now!

And your daughter must know that girls who are more beautiful than her are waiting in a long queue for Bigvy, and Bigvy never sheds a damn tear for a cheap bitch playing big in a small township!'

'Mr Masemola ... Mr Masemola,' said Rolivhuwa's mother, 'Please put your heart down. I appreciate your anger, but please don't leave this house in an angry mood. My enemies and witches can celebrate! Whenever your car stops at my gate I feel proud for I'm the envy of the street. Now when my next-door neighbours see that you are upset as you leave my house, the busy-bodies are going to find work, and we are going to be the laughing stock of the whole section of Mamelodi.'

Bigvy sighed. 'I wish your daughter could appreciate that.' He no longer sounded angry.

'Yes, Mr Masemola. I told her she must count her blessings.'

'*Mamazala*, you are lucky I'm not a *tsotsi* type. Otherwise I would bang the door and kick the table shouting: *Where's your daughter? Bring her out, or I stab you to death*!'

'Mr Masemola, please be patient with my daughter. If you really love her, please have a big heart.'

'I have a big heart, *mamazala*, but I don't want to be treated like a big fool. As things are now, I'm not sure if I've been made to hold the feathers while the bird is gone.'

Rolivhuwa's mother laughed. It was the first time

that she heard her mother laughing in that manner in the presence of Bigvy.

'Mr Masemola, you still have the bird.'

'Really?'

'Yes. The bird can return to you any moment, Mr Masemola. Please be patient, sir. A girl of 18 is still a child; you'll have to raise her for yourself. This often happens when you are courting a very young woman.'

'Do you think that parting with part of the lobola for her will be a good idea? Perhaps she'll be better controlled than if she's a free bird?' he asked.

Her mother chuckled. 'I don't know Mr Masemola ...'

'She doesn't know what wonderful things are waiting for her, *mamazala*. I intend to plan for us a week-long honeymoon in Mauritius, and I will later buy her a very expensive sports car, a red Porsche Boxter, new from the box!'

'You know, Mr Masemola, our people sometimes say to walk is better than to run.'

Bigvy grinned. 'I'm with you, *mamazala*.'

Relieved to hear two pairs of footsteps leaving the house, Rolivhuwa hissed, 'Hamba sugar daddy!'

She stifled a laugh, thrilled that her trick had worked for the second time. She also heard Bigvy's BMW driving away. She could picture him sour-faced turning the powered steering wheel towards the main street. Her mother's footsteps entered the house and the door closed. Footsteps faded to her mother's bedroom.

'Oh Jehovah of peace!' her mother sighed and smashed her palms together. 'Why must unfortunate things happen to me? I was the envy of the whole township, now if Mr Masemola ditches Rolivhuwa, and he takes away the furniture, her clothes, the cellphone, the computer and other things, we shall be laughed at even by nursing infants and the birds. He'll no longer address me as *mamazala* but a witch! Oh Jehovah of peace, help my daughter to come to her senses, Amen!'

Suddenly her mother heard the sound of the wardrobe door squeaking open from her daughter's bedroom.

'Oh Jehovah of peace, what's happening now?' she walked slowly towards Rolivhuwa's bedroom. 'Is there a *tokoloshe* in my house?'

11

Rolivhuwa straightened up herself, put her hands on her waist and stood with her feet apart. Mother and daughter faced each other, as if one of them was making the statement: *If you are a tiger, I'm a leopard!*

'Strange things are happening in this house, Mama,' said Rolivhuwa softly, 'Your daughter has become a *tokoloshe.*'

'Don't be silly, Vhovho! Come let's sit in the lounge and talk.'

In order to diffuse tension Rolivhuwa made tea and the two sipped as they talked.

'Vhovho, I'm shocked that you are capable of doing such a thing. Why are you doing such a thing to such a good guy? You are really forcing him to look for other girls, Vhovho!'

'Let him have other girls. After all, he's having them anyway. I must check my HIV status.'

'You know, Vhovho, my grandmother often said that when a springhare doesn't want a hole it will enter it in reverse so that it must have an excuse for leaving the hole, saying it is no longer good for my hair.'

'I really don't understand what you are trying to tell me, Mama. Are you saying I'm just trying to find an excuse? Anyway, you shouldn't be shocked, because I prepared you a week ago. Haven't I said that I don't want him to touch me any longer?'

'Yes, you said that, but I thought you would nevertheless follow my motherly advice.'

'I'm not prepared to continue to sacrifice my principles.'

'I'm certain you've heard Mr Masemola saying that he's considering to part with lobola for you. This means you'll no longer be sleeping with him for money. He will be grooming you as his next junior wife. If he has money and he can give you a comfortable life, why can't you accept the offer? The good thing is, Mr Masemola is prepared to help you to realise your dream. He has promised to buy you a car, hasn't he?'

'I'm no longer interested. And what makes you think that if he parts with lobola for me he will stop being someone's sugar daddy? The girl who introduced me to bra Bigvy once told me to enjoy the sweet life of having a sugar daddy, but I've come to realise that there is a bitter after-taste.'

'Who said life will be sweet all the time? Vhovho, are you aware that you are taking food out of my mouth?'

'How am I doing that?'

'I'll explain that to you.' Her mother became tearful. 'You don't seem to see the consequences of your action.'

'What consequences?'

'Listen Vhovho, why don't you count your blessing instead of …?'

'What you refer to as blessings are in fact honey that sweetens the poison.'

'What poison? Listen Vhovho. You know what Mr Masemola is going to do if you leave him?'

'I don't care!'

'You don't care that he's going to take away the furniture, your clothes and your cellphone?'

'Let him take them! I would rather be poor, living in peace than live in riches without peace. Let him take them!'

'How am I going to face people if…?'

'Let him take them!'

'How am I going to face people who used to congratulate me for having given birth to a daughter who has won the heart of a rich man? People are going to laugh at us when they see a truck taking away the furniture.'

'Let them laugh! You don't have to impress people at my expense, Mama! Let him go! Hamba sugar daddy!'

'Vhovho, how can you speak like that? I told many people about how good Mr Masemola is. I have been saying: "God doesn't give directly with His hand; He uses other people." Now people are going to laugh at me and say: "God has changed his mind. He is taking back what He has given."'

Her mother continued to sob and Rolivhuwa tried to comfort her.

* * *

After supper Rolivhuwa prepared tea and served her mother. She washed the dishes and then went out to the garden to make a call on her cellphone. When she returned she told her mother that she had decided to go to sleep early and that she wanted to wake up early so that she could get busy with her studies. Her mother wanted to know who she had been speaking to for over half an hour, but she decided to keep her mouth shut, for peace's sake.

* * *

It was Sunday morning. When her mother awoke at six, a thought crossed her mind: *Make peace with your daughter before you go to church.* When she entered Rolivhuwa's room she was shocked to find it empty. She put on the light and looked around the room. She hurried to the bathroom where she knocked.

'Vhovho!' she called.

There was no response. She opened the door. Walking into the kitchen, her eyes were drawn to a handwritten note, stuck with Prestik to the back of the door. When she saw 'Dear Mama' written on top, she knew it was a letter from Rolivhuwa.

For the sake of sanity and peace, I have decided to leave this house and go and stay with one of my relatives. When I called her last night she said I could come and stay with them; she said she would rather bedevil the relationship between you and her than allow a situation where a mother encourages her daughter to continue sleeping with a sugar daddy for financial and material gain. I'm sorry to have shocked you by taking this bold step of leaving the comfort of my home.

With love from Vhovho

She re-read the letter before she folded it. *So she has gone to stay with Bertha!* She spoke aloud. *She's my younger sister but she behaves as if she's my elder sister. When everybody appreciated Vhovho's birthday party, she was against it because she said the idea of a sugar daddy nauseates her. She behaves like a pastor's wife! Because she has no children she wants to take Vhovho as her own daughter. I'll go to her house and I'll tell her in front of her husband: Shit your own baby!* She suddenly put her hand on her mouth. *Oh, no I mustn't speak like this when I'm about to go to the house of the Lord.*

Rolivhuwa's mother sighed and beat her palms together. *Oh Jehovah of peace!* She continued to speak to herself aloud. *Why must strange things happen to me again? I was the envy of the whole township.*

When Mr Masemola mentioned that he was prepared to buy her a car during Vhovho's birthday party, and also help to pay for her school fees, I said in my heart: 'Hallelujah! God has seen my tears and heard and answered my prayers!' I started to count my blessings. Now everything is falling apart. Vhovho is no longer interested in Mr Masemola. Oh Jehovah of peace, help my daughter to come to her senses, Amen!

12

On Monday, Rolivhuwa and Kedibone didn't get a chance to speak to each other; each one of them was constantly being mobbed by admirers. They kept sneaking looks at each other. Although it was clear from their body language that they were eager to speak to each other, neither of them took the initiative. After school, Rolivhuwa was walking out of the gate with the last group of girls when she saw Bigvy's car.

Her heart skipped a beat and she gasped. She stopped suddenly and the two girls who were on either side of her continued walking. She took out her cellphone and pretended to be checking messages. When she raised her head she saw Bigvy, grinning and waving a bunch of red carnations towards her. Her heart was softened; her resistance began to thaw and dissolved completely within seconds. As a result she found herself smiling as if all her knowledge regarding her relationship with Bigvy thus far had been erased and had been replaced by new data. *Has bra Bigvy used a vela-ba-hleke charm to soften my heart?* She asked herself as she opened the door and sat beside the man she had vowed she never wanted to meet again.

Her heart was now filled with a mixture of affection and even pity towards Bigvy. Bigvy drove and she never asked where they were going. It was as if they had agreed on the destination. The car was heading towards Pretoria city centre. The face and tone of Bigvy's voice never revealed any malice. He never asked why Rolivhuwa had evaded her on Saturday. He behaved as if nothing had happened. All he said was: 'Babe, let's go somewhere where we can relax and talk.' She didn't ask exactly where.

He parked beside a hotel. 'Roli, my apple-tart, let's have a drink and snacks.'

Thirty minutes later, he said: 'I want us to go to an office on the sixth floor. There are offices that can be hired for one-to-one business meetings; they can be used by those who want to use proper desks and other office equipment.'

She asked no questions, so she walked beside him to take a lift to the sixth floor. He unlocked the door, stepped backward and allowed her to enter first. When she looked around and saw two beds, she realised she had been tricked. Bigvy locked the room and grinned. She gave him a faint smile and sat on a couch next to the bed. He removed his shoes.

'Thank you for behaving like a lady,' Bigvy's smile lingered on his face.

'Thanks for the complement, bra Big.'

He gave her a grin that matured into a smile. 'And babe, if you cooperate, I'll buy you a red Porsche Boxter.'

'Really?'

'Yes!' His smile faded away. 'Now, let's talk business. Roli, you are a clever girl of the city. You aren't a dull girl of the village. You know that there is what is called sponsorship. A sponsor spends money, but he expects something in return. Absa spends millions on soccer matches, but what are they getting? Business. So I'm sponsoring you in many ways: I've transformed your mother's *mokhukhu* into a five-roomed house with expensive roof-tiles, and I've furnished it.

'Today you are the proud owner of an iPhone 4s 16GB, you have nice clothes, airtime, monthly supplies of cosmetics, and you are a beautiful girl. You were poor girl who couldn't afford *sphatlo*; today you can afford chicken and rice every day. Your mother was having *malana le dikilana, dihlogwana le maotwana* for lunch, today she can afford high-quality chicken, lamb and pork.

'You were a plain girl but today you are a *smatsatsa*, and you're attracting the attention of teachers and boys. And you want to leave me and go for a boy or teacher of your fancy? You aren't going to do that, Roli! Bigvy isn't a *moegoe* who will plant a tree, fertilise, water it and wait for another man to come, pluck and eat the delicious fruit. No, that's not going to happen to Bigvy.'

He pointed a finger at her, 'Bigvy takes no shit! So come, undress and let me have sex until I'm satisfied! I've not taken the African Viagra for nothing!'

He unbuttoned his shirt, unbuckled his belt and pushed his trousers to his knees.

'Roli, what are you waiting for? If you can't undress yourself I will do it for you! If you resist I can tear your panties, bra and dress and buy you new and better ones.'

He removed his trousers and stood with a semi-erect penis. She folded her arms and put on a mask of nonchalance and defiance. She was still standing, fully clothed. She looked through the window, thinking about how she could escape from the sugar daddy she cared nothing about.

'I'm your only sponsor, now's the time for me to continue getting my share of sex. If I want to have sex, you can't tell me that because of what you call PMT, I can't have sex. No, that can't happen to Bigvy. Bigvy takes no bullshit. The sponsor has all the right and privilege of getting what he wants from the sponsored person, when he wants.

'Can you imagine Kaizer Chiefs or Orlando Pirates teams telling Absa: "We don't feel like playing today." Absa will say: "You are talking rubbish Kaizer Chiefs, I'm sponsoring you! So play now!" Money talks, and he who has the means calls the shots. So I'm saying: "I'm sponsoring you Roli, so sex now!" I spoil you, you spoil me! Come, undress and romance me now. Thereafter we shall get into bed and I shall have sex as long as I want, until this African Viagra runs out of power!

'I'm giving you money and other things; you eat me,

you shit me, you sleep me, so you are my property, and I'll sleep with you when I want, not when you want!'

She was still standing with her arms crossed, wearing a frown; she turned away from him. He walked to her, grabbed her, turned her face to face him and shook her. He gripped her school uniform from behind her shoulder, tore it off, and threw it on the floor.

Bigvy breathed heavily. 'If this is what you are looking for, you'll get it!'

He looked deep into her eyes. 'Now remove your shoes and romance me now!'

She made no move and stood still. He pushed her backwards and she fell on the carpet and sat on her buttocks; he removed her black school shoes.

He opened his arms and caressed her 'Okay, I'm going to romance you!'

She pushed him away and got up. He stepped closer to her; when she tried to push him again he grabbed her hands and twisted her right arms. She screamed.

'Shut up, bitch!'

He tried to caress her but she resisted him; he slapped her and then punched her in the right eye, hard enough to knock her to the floor.

'Now you are coming to bed, you are going to lie on your back and open your thighs. I'm going to romance you, and insert my *ntoto* into you, and you are going to smile and enjoy sex as I help myself, okay?'

Wearing only a sleeveless vest he squatted between her open thighs, ready to penetrate her with an erect penis, proudly displaying veins amok with libido. She lifted her legs, bent her thighs towards her breast and also bent her neck a little towards her thighs.

'Can we try a different style today,' said Rolivhuwa.

Bigvy was utterly impressed with how she was cooperating.

As Bigvy was tightening his penis with his right hand, ready to penetrate her, she suddenly unleashed a powerful double-kick with her heels, aimed at his bulging stomach, and he fell on his back, groaning. She stood up and screamed with all the air in her lungs.

'Shut up, you fucken bitch!'

She continued to run around the room screaming: 'Iyooo! Please help! Someone is killing me! Iyooo! Please help!'

Bigvy stopped chasing her and instantaneously put on his trousers and his shirt. There was a loud knock at the door. Rolivhuwa hurriedly put on her bra and wrapped the lower part of her body with a towel.

13

'Open or we break the door!' hollered someone behind the door.

Bigvy turned the latch and the door was flung open. The hotel security guard leapt into the room holding a gun which he turned from right to left, his hawk eyes sharp. A second security guard stepped into the room, wielding a club. Bigvy lifted up his arms, and the guard holding a club handcuffed him. Rolivhuwa sat on the couch, sobbing, as the two guards led Bigvy out of the room. But she suddenly stopped crying and hastened towards the door.

She pointed with her index finger, hissing, 'Hamba sugar daddy! We shall meet in court!'

Members of SAPS arrived later. Two police women took a statement from Rolivhuwa. Two hours later social workers attached to SAPS came to interview Rolivhuwa.

* * *

Bertha, Rolivhuwa's mother's younger sister, who was working in the city, took Rolivhuwa to a medical centre where she was treated for a bruised eye. Her mother arrived at the medical centre and met Rolivhuwa and Bertha on the ground floor, as they emerged from the lift.

'I'm sorry that this has happened to you, Vhovho,' said her mother. 'But what have you done to cause him to raise a hand?'

'So you want to put the blame on me? Go and ask angel Bigvy!'

'Vhovho, lovers have fights at times, my girl. So please cancel the case. We can discuss this problem at home as Africans.'

'Go and cancel the case!' said Rolivhuwa icily.

'Let's go,' said Bertha, 'let's not cause a spectacle in public.'

'Now where is Vhovho going from here?' Rolivhuwa's mother asked Bertha, 'are you taking her to your house?'

'She must decide where she wants to go.'

'I'm going with you, Aunt Bertha,' said Rolivhuwa.

'It's all right, Bertha. Keep my daughter at your house, and you can also have her lobola money when ...'

'Oh shut up, Mama!' snapped Rolivhuwa.

'No, please don't speak like that to your mother,' chided Bertha. 'She deserves all your respect, even if she is in the wrong.'

'I'm sorry, Aunt Bertha.'

'*Ausi* Regina,' said Bertha softly. 'Vhovho is your daughter, and she'll return to her home when she has recovered, and when she's ready to stay with you. At the moment, there's still a lot of tension between the two of you. Perhaps a social worker could help to restore a harmonious relationship.'

Rolivhuwa told Bertha and her mother that the social worker had advised her to do HIV tests. So they walked to the city clinic for the tests.

* * *

On Tuesday, Rolivhuwa could not go to school. Kedibone heard from Guff that Rolivhuwa had laid a charge of assault against Bigvy. On Wednesday morning Rolivhuwa went to school very early; she was the first learner to arrive. She walked straight to her classroom and tried to catch up on what she had missed. Fortunately, her accounting teacher, Mr Malebogo, had written his notes on the board, so Rolivhuwa took notes and also referred to her text book.

Classmates who arrived in twos and threes wanted to know why she had missed school the previous day. She had to make up a story, that her jealous former boyfriend tried to assault her and that she hit a wall as she was running away. From their facial expressions Rolivhuwa knew that they knew that she was lying. All her teachers were pleased to see her back in class.

During break, Rolivhuwa rushed to the toilets and returned quickly to her class. She saw Kedibone but she pretended not to have seen her. Minutes later, as Rolivhuwa was busy with her books, Kedibone knocked and then entered the classroom.

'*Hau, chomi ya ka,*' said Kedibone, forcing a smile.

Rolivhuwa stood up. 'You call me, *chomi ya ka?*'

Kedibone kept walking slowly down the aisle towards Rolivhuwa's desk.

Rolivhuwa pointed to the door. 'Out!'

'*Hau* Rolis, are you in a bad mood today?'

Rolivhuwa waved a forefinger. 'I said, get out!'

'No, don't do that to me, Roli. What are our enemies going to think when they see us fighting? We are going to be the laughing stock.'

Rolivhuwa got up and walked briskly towards the green board and Kedibone retreated hurriedly. Rolivhuwa took a piece of chalk, bent down and drew a line.

'You cross this line, I break you neck!' shouted Rolivhuwa.

Kedibone stood at the doorway facing Rolivhuwa. She paced slowly towards Rolivhuwa. '*Chomi ya ka,* please let's talk!'

Rolivhuwa pointed to Kedibone. 'Bitch, I told you to stay away from me!' Kedibone retreated and stood at the doorway and folded her arms. 'I'm in this mess because of you!' hissed Rolivhuwa.

'*Eish*! How dare you speak to me like that? You should count your blessings instead of ...' responded Kedibone.

'What blessings? That was poison which sweetened ...'

'What poison?'

'Listen, you are the one who dropped the idea of a sugar daddy into my head! You and Guff organised Bigvy for me, and you've been my coach to drink wine. You once told me to enjoy the sweet life of having a sugar daddy, but I'm realising now that there is a bitter aftertaste.'

Kedibone frowned. 'Have I opened your mouth and forced you to drink wine? Have I opened your thighs and put Bigvy on top of you?' Kedibone scowled. 'This is very funny! Instead of thanking me for introducing you to an exciting life of having better things, you are blaming me. You should be thanking me, instead of ...'

'Thanking you for ruining my life?'

'Haven't you enjoyed stacks of money, nice clothes, a fancy iPhone, other wonderful things? Bigvy has also extended your mother's house and furnished it; you and your mother *le ja soft*. I don't understand you, Roli. You call a good life poison. What has got into your head?

'Your mother is right: you should focus on your blessings and not on a problem. You should have continued to be a blessee and make a lot out of the bastard. Bigvy was about to enter the third level as a blesser, where he would take you on holidays to exotic destinations such as Mauritius. And I heard that he is planning to buy you an expensive car called a Porsche Boxter. Now you ...'

'I don't care about all those ...!'

'You know my grandpa often said a black man's thank you is a *voetsek*!'

By this point, many students were standing at the door behind Kedibone, while others peered through the windows, with smiles and grins, others making faces and clearly enjoying the verbal duel. Kedibone walked to her classroom while Rolivhuwa sat back down at her desk.

14

The following day during break Khomisa went to Rolivhuwa's classroom and asked to sit with her while they ate. As they were eating and speaking Rolivhuwa could see Kedibone standing a distance away, and she was distracted for a moment.

'Please continue,' said Khomisa.

After listening attentively to Rolivhuwa, Khomisa said: 'You did a sensible thing by getting out of the sugar daddy relationship. You are lucky ... let me put it this way: Thanks to God's grace you got out of the devil's dirty hands. Many girls remain trapped forever because of the sugar daddies' evil tricks of manipulation, intimidation and bribery of parents.'

'Thank you for your words of encouragement, Khomi.'

'But be ready for what's lying ahead of you, Roli. The devil isn't going to fold his filthy hands and leave you in peace. *Aowa*! Like Pharaoh's army trying to overtake and capture the Israelites, the devil is going to give chase. But we are going to pray for you, and one day we shall see Pharaoh's army drowning in the Red Sea.'

'I'll be delighted to see that happening Khomi.'

Khomisa stepped closer to Rolivhuwa and gave her a firm hug.

'You know, Roli,' said Khomisa with a sweet smile, 'You have really ...'

Khomisa saw two student leaders standing behind Rolivhuwa.

'Sorry to interrupt,' said the Students' Representative Council president, Sibusiso Mnisi, standing with his deputy Dikeledi Mathe.

'No problem,' said Rolivhuwa.

'Can we speak to you after school?' inquired Sibusiso.

'You are most welcome, S'bu.'

Sibusiso and Dikeledi walked away.

'I was saying you have really taken a bold step,' Khomisa continued, 'and I want to congratulate you for your guts.'

'Thank you, Khomi. I'm just concerned with one thing: I have taken an HIV test and I'm hoping that I won't be HIV positive.'

'I'll pray for you, Roli. You remind me of the story of the prodigal son. It's that story in the Bible in the book of Luke. One morning the son woke up and said to himself: "I'll arise and go to my father and say to him, *Father I have sinned against heaven and before you.*" Roli, the best way of resisting the devil is to be a child of God.'

At that moment the school bell rang. 'It's alright Roli, let's talk next time.'

* * *

After school, Rolivhuwa found Sibusiso and Dikeledi at a classroom that was used by the 'night school' adult learners. They were with another student.

'Roli,' said Sibusiso, who gestured towards the boy, 'meet Matsobane Makola. He's in Grade 12C.'

Rolivhuwa and Matsobane shook hands.

'Roli, we know, or let me say, we have an idea about what you are going through,' said Sibusiso, 'and we want to assure you that we are behind you.'

'Thank you, S'bu.'

'We care about you and other girls who are caught up in sugar daddy relationships,' said Dikeledi.

'Matsobane has an interesting project,' said Sibusiso. 'Over to you, Tsubi!'

'I've written a script about sugar daddies and sugar babies,' said Matsobane.

Rolivhuwa raised her eyebrows and smiled.

'Last year when I was in Grade 11, my English teacher asked us to write a short play. At that time my elder sister had bought a women's magazine in which I found an article about sugar daddies. As I read the article, I just felt it would make an interesting sketch. In addition to the article I know of a few girls who are dating men old enough to be their fathers.

'I've brought together a group of drama lovers who are in Grades 11 and 12; I am the director. We've been rehearsing for a month. We want to go to the principal and ask to perform the sketch at school. If it's successful we can perhaps go and perform it at the community hall, for the benefit of learners from other high schools.'

'That's a terrific idea!' enthused Rolivhuwa.

'And we want you to give directorial input later. Would you be available?' inquired Matsobane.

'Of course!'

15

Rolivhuwa felt dizzy and she was tearful as she stepped out of the AIDS counsellor's office at the city council's central clinic. She trudged along the busy pavement, her head down. Her gait was weak and she felt like she needed crutches. She understood why the SMS from the nurse had said: *Please come with a close relative or a friend.* Her aunt, Bertha, was not available because it was stock-taking day at the pharmaceutical company where she was employed. Kedibone was no longer her friend. She wished she should have asked Khomisa, whose Christian principles would make a difference. She pulled herself together until she arrived in Church Street, now renamed Stanza Bopape, from where she boarded a taxi back to Mamelodi.

She was depressed throughout the taxi trip. All she was thinking was: *So I can die any moment!* She had completely forgotten the words of the AIDS counsellor that being HIV positive did not mean that she had a death sentence hanging over her head. The counsellor had given her all sorts of advice including exercises, diet and a positive attitude. *If you can use your religious beliefs as an anchor, the better,* advised the nurse.

When Rolivhuwa saw students from several schools in the city standing in groups and chatting excitedly, moving about, skipping and chasing each other, she thought: *so they'll be attending my funeral!* She could see a funeral procession: a hearse carrying her coffin followed by a family car, three busloads full of former classmates, and many cars, all driving slowly, flashing their hazard lights ... Her train of thought was interrupted by a hand touching her shoulder: a passenger was giving her the coins and notes she had collected to be passed to the driver.

When she arrived at her aunt's place she walked straight to her bedroom. She had no appetite; the nurse had advised her to start eating salads. She wanted to call Khomisa, but she was in no mood to talk to anyone. All she wanted was to rest on her bed, hoping that sleep would transport her from the gnawing thoughts of misery. She had hardly been asleep for an hour when she heard her cellphone registering an incoming message. She glanced at the cellphone screen; the message was from Khomisa. *Did it go well?* She replied: *No!* Her cellphone rang.

'Can I come over to your place now?' asked Khomisa.

'Yes please,' she said tearfully, suppressing a sob.

'Please SMS me the directions.'

'I'll do that.'

* * *

Khomisa arrived thirty minutes later. They sat in the lounge.

'Thanks for coming, Khomi,' Rolivhuwa looked at Khomisa with blood-shot eyes. 'Khomi ... Khomi ... I ... I ...' she broke down in tears. 'I'm HIV positive.'

Khomisa went to sit beside her, gave her a warm hug and rubbed her shoulder. Rolivhuwa buried her face in her hands and continued to sob painfully.

'I'm sorry to hear about that,' said Khomisa softly.

'He said he would help me to realise my dream. I trusted him. Now look at what he has done! My future is in tatters now, and I will soon die!'

'No, you won't die, Roli!'

'I hate him!'

'No, don't do that. Hate is self-destructive.'

Khomisa continued to brush Rolivhuwa's shoulders; she stopped crying and looked down to her feet, in deep thought, for a long while.

Rolivhuwa turned her face towards Khomisa. 'You promised to pray for me, Khomi. Why hasn't God heard your prayer? And tomorrow I'm writing the accounting quarterly test. How can I write in this state of mind?'

Rolivhuwa bent her head and began to shed more tears. Khomisa handed her a tissue and she wiped her tears and blew her nose.

'You know, Roli, God is a specialist who turns negatives into positives.'

'Is there anything positive in me being HIV positive?'

'In my human mind I can say, no, but in His eyes and attitude all things are possible. He is able to draw water from a rock, and a tragedy into a triumph.'

They spent the next thirty minutes without talking. Khomisa was brushing the back of Rolivhuwa's hand. Khomisa took out yoghurt she had brought with and they shared it. Rolivhuwa told her about the history of her relationship with Bigvy and her friendship with Kedibone.

'When the relationship with that sugar daddy started, I looked forward to enjoying a sweet life but all I'm getting now is a bitter aftertaste.'

'I can assure you one thing Roli, if you come to God, He will replace that bitter aftertaste with the real sweetness of honey.' Khomisa reminded Rolivhuwa of the nursing sister who had advised her to lean on religious beliefs.

With tears still glinting in her eyes, Rolivhuwa smiled. 'Thank you, Khomi, for your positive words that really give me hope.'

'You are most welcome, Roli. We are on this planet not to live for ourselves only, but to share our lives with fellow human beings.'

'Thank you, Khomi. And please forgive me for all those unkind words I have said to you when you ...'

'It's all right, Roli. I could have done the same thing if I were in your situation.'

Khomisa opened her palms and high-fived her.

* * *

Three teachers told Rolivhuwa that they were disappointed with her performance during the September quarterly tests.

Her accounting teacher, Meneer Malebogo, spoke to her before she went home after school.

'Rolivhuwa, I'm very concerned with your poor performance.' Malebogo pointed to a sheet in front of him, 'You are one of my best students in accounting. Your marks were 78% in first quarter, 80%, second quarter and now it's 48%. How do I explain this to the HoD? What can you tell me?'

'Sir, I'm very disappointed that I've received 48%.'

'I have no doubt something has gone seriously wrong. What is it? Please don't tell me. I suggest that you speak to the guidance teacher, mma-Legodi.'

16

The following afternoon, Rolivhuwa was sitting in front of mma-Legodi. The last time she had spoken to her guidance teacher was when she had asked about the meaning of 'sugar baby'. Rolivhuwa could still recall what mma-Legodi said that day: *In this sexual relationship the older is perceived as the richer, and is known as the 'sugar daddy', and the younger of the two is called 'sugar baby'.*

Mma-Legodi smiled at Rolivhuwa and said, 'You know what you want to tell me, so please do so.'

Rolivhuwa told mma-Legodi how the relationship with Bigvy started and how it culminated in him leaving her with a black eye. She also disclosed that she was HIV positive. Mma-Legodi listened attentively, asking a few questions to get clarity.

'Thank you, Roli, for sharing your story of success with me. Yes, it's a story of success! Because you took initiative by ending your relationship with a sugar daddy.'

'Thank you, ma'am,' said Rolivhuwa tearfully.

'What I can also say is, don't look backward like Lot's wife. Be focused on your dream. Avoid bad company, and surround yourself with people who will add value to your life.'

'Thank you, ma'am.'

'And I want to encourage you to see what you now call a problem as an opportunity.'

'Will you please explain, ma'am?'

'Let me complicate it before I explain it: on the flip side of the problem waits an opportunity. There are many examples I can give you. The manager of a successful company was fired and he was depressed and angry for days until his wife said to him, "Why don't you start your own company, instead of crying over something that you can't change?" The man said "Yaa-neéh!" and he then started to work on a business proposal.

'Five years later when his business was successful, he went to his former boss and said, "Mr Van Schalkwyk, thank you for firing me five years ago!" What we see here is a blessing in disguise. So it's for you to look at the back of the problem to see an opportunity. What do you think about what I've just told you?'

'I never thought of my problem as an opportunity; it makes sense the way you are explaining it, ma'am.'

'You told me your problem, so what are your opportunities?'

Rolivhuwa considered the question for a short while. She grinned. 'I don't know, Ma'am. Will you please help me?'

'No, I'm not going to spoon-feed you. Let it be your homework.'

'It's all right, Ma'am.'

'And by the way, what is your dream?'

'To be a CA.'

'Great! Next time I want us to talk about how to achieve your dream.'

'I'll appreciate it very much, Ma'am.'

* * *

The afternoon before the court hearing, Rolivhuwa walked towards the classroom for adult learners. She saw mma-Legodi walking to the car park and she rushed to her.

'Ma'am,' said Rolivhuwa, 'I've done my homework about the opportunity that comes from my problem. Because of my problem of being HIV positive, I can be an AIDS/HIV counsellor.'

'Excellent!'

'My experience as a sugar baby is providing me with an opportunity to be a peer counsellor of girls trapped in sugar daddy affairs. I can also be a speaker, visiting various schools to spread the message that being a sugar baby has serious consequences.'

'Fantastic!'

Rolivhuwa hastened towards the building where she found Sibusiso, Matsobane and Dikeledi waiting.

'Regarding the court hearing, we want to assure you that we are ready to support you by attending in huge numbers,' said Sibusiso.

'Thanks, guys.'

'We want to send a strong message that an injury to one is an injury to all,' said Dikeledi.

'Great, guys!' Rolivhuwa turned towards Matsobane, 'How did the meeting with the headmaster go?'

'He's very excited about the idea of the sketch. He said we are doing the right project at the right time,' said Matsobane. 'The drama group is busy rehearsing the sketch. Would you be able to attend?'

Rolivhuwa chuckled, 'Yes of course! What is the title of the sketch?' inquired Rolivhuwa.

'Hamba Sugar Daddy!'

Rolivhuwa chortled.

'Why are you laughing?'

'I'm just intrigued by the title.' Rolivhuwa continued to laugh.

'Come, let's go and see it,' said Matsobane.

Rolivhuwa, Sibusiso, Matsobane and Dikeledi

found six members of the Students' Representative Council sitting in the front row waiting for the sketch to begin. Matsobane gave the performers the cue to start by switching off the lights.

The sketch lasted only 20 minutes. At the end, Matsobane went to the front to bow with the aspiring actors and actresses. The one-row audience applauded, with Rolivhuwa clapping enthusiastically.

'It's a very short sketch,' said Matsobane, 'because we want to have time for a group discussion.'

'I must say I'm thoroughly fascinated by the idea,' said Rolivhuwa, wiping a tear. 'And I can see it's very informative.'

'Thank you, Roli,' said Matsobane.

'It must be seen by learners and parents,' Rolivhuwa added. 'I can relate to the play.'

'Great! Do you have any input?' asked Matsobane.

'Yes. It's the part where the girl cries when she tells her mother that she wants to leave the sugar daddy. It can be improved; let the girl raise her voice, and let's see real tears, if possible. If we can't see tears let's feel the pain! Let me come to the mother. She says: "If you leave *ntate* Mavundla he will ask us to give back the lounge suite, and our neighbours are going to laugh at us when they see him carrying the furniture out of the house." I want to suggest that more drama should be added by having mother and daughter pointing at each and perhaps even wrestling with each other.'

'Great contribution!' said Matsobane.

'Now what's the future of the play?' Rolivhuwa inquired.

'We plan to perform it at the Mamelodi Civic Centre just before we write exams. We are going to ask our principal to speak to other headmasters and ask them to send bus-loads of learners to the venue.'

'It's a brilliant idea,' said Rolivhuwa.

Matsobane gave Rolivhuwa a wry smile. 'Roli, why don't you become part of the sketch, by playing the leading role?'

Rolivhuwa laughed aloud. 'Are you serious Tsubi?'

'Yes. You have a passion for the play, and through your personal experience you can help us to present a winning play!'

'I think Tsubi is right, you should have the leading role,' said Dikeledi.

Sibusiso nodded.

'Guys, I've a lot to do as a Grade 12 learner,' said Rolivhuwa. 'Will I have time for the play?'

'You can do it, Roli,' said Sibusiso.

'I'll help you to catch up with other performers,' said Matsobane.

Rolivhuwa shrugged her shoulders, smiling. 'Okay, I'll take up the challenge.'

Matsobane handed Rolivhuwa the script.

17

That Friday morning the SRC had bargained and negotiated with the principal that they would go to court and lend support to their fellow student, Rolivhuwa, who was waiting at the court. They had agreed with the headmaster that they would attend lessons on Saturday to compensate for learning time lost. What they did not tell the headmaster was that they had invited fellow learners from other high schools in the township.

By 8:30am thousands of students wearing their school uniforms had congregated at an empty plot opposite the court where they chanted, waving placards written: *To Hell with sugar daddy Bigvy; We support U Roli; Sugar daddies, your days are numbered.*

Rolivhuwa was sitting at the benches in front of Court C. Her mother had told her that she would not come with her because Rolivhuwa was disobeying her by refusing to cancel the case. The previous night Bigvy came to her home and showed her a stack of banknotes, saying: 'If you withdraw the case, this money is yours!' Her mother tried to persuade her to accept Bigvy's money, but she was adamant that the case should go on.

Rolivhuwa did not see Bigvy anywhere in or around the court building, but she saw an Indian man wearing a suit talking to the prosecutor; she assumed that the man was Bigvy's lawyer. She waited until noon, she was informed that the case had been postponed indefinitely because the docket was missing.

At that moment three student leaders arrived and told her that she should come immediately to speak to the students whose patience was wearing thinner and thinner. The leaders led her to the back of a bakkie where another student leader was holding a megaphone. Rolivhuwa climbed onto the bakkie and took the megaphone. She told the students what had happened. An angry student jumped into the van and grabbed the megaphone out of Rolivhuwa's hands.

'We demand justice!' said the student, 'and we want to say to the corrupt court official: "Bring back that docket within 24 hours, or else we are going to burn the court buildings!"'

The students applauded.

Subisiso took the megaphone. 'No, we aren't going to resort to violent tactics. And we aren't going to imitate the strategy of some of our parents and older brothers who burn tyres, barricade the roads, stone passing cars and burn clinics, libraries and schools. What madness! No, we aren't going to do that! No ways!'

The students applauded.

'But we are going to demand fair justice through peaceful means.'

At that moment a crew from Mamelodi TV arrived at the scene and asked to interview Rolivhuwa. The student leaders cooperated, and Rolivhuwa was given a huge microphone.

'Roli, what are you learning from this situation?' inquired the journalist, a young woman in her twenties, wearing jeans.

'My lesson is that sugar daddy dating is like poison mixed with honey: something that now tastes sweet, kills a moment later!'

The students applauded uproariously.

'So what's your advice to sugar babies?'

Rolivhuwa lifted her right hand and raised a forefinger. 'One! Young women, don't fall for the trap of the so-called blessers. Don't envy sugar babies who seem to have nice things such as expensive cellphones, expensive clothes and money. There is nothing for *mahala*. These girls are paying a huge price. They pay with their bodies, and most of them have AIDS as *pasela*. Other girls risk death in the hands of illegal abortionists. For a short moment you enjoy something sweet, but there is a bitter aftertaste. Young women, choose to stay poor rather than sell your bodies to these old stinking men for quick money.'

The students applauded again.

Rolivhuwa lifted her middle finger. 'Two! Don't be misled by celebrity sugar babies such as Khanyi Mbalula who appear smiling in newspapers and on TV screens. They are their sugar daddies' trophy girls.

All you see is a beautiful picture, but the ugly side is hidden from your eyes.'

Another loud applause followed.

'And I have a word for you sugar daddies. If you claim to be helping needy girls, why must you be rewarded by sleeping with them?'

The audience clapped their hands.

'Any word for the parents?' the TV interviewer asked Rolivhuwa.

'To the parents, I want to say: "Don't allow yourselves to be seduced by money and material things from your daughters' sugar daddies! No! When every weekend your daughter comes home with a braai pack, don't pretend not to see what's happening. You know that there is a sugar daddy behind that. I have heard that the youngest blessees are 14 or 15 years old, and this is happening with the knowledge and encouragement of the parents. Parents, stop abusing your children. Get the bastards arrested for statutory rape!"'

Again the students clapped their hands lustily.

As the TV crew left, Sibusiso, the SRC president, stood on the back of the bakkie holding a megaphone. '*Phanzi* with sugar daddies, *phanzi*!' Sibusiso shouted.

'*Phanzii*!!' responded the students.

'*Phambili* with girls who want education first, *phambili*!'

'*Phambili*!!'

'*Phanzii* with girls after sugar daddies, *phanzi*!!'

'*Phanzii*!!'

'*Phambili* with girls who are the pride of the nation, *phambili*!'

'*Phambili*!!'

'Fellow students, we are launching an anti-sugar daddy march. We are going to make a bold statement with our feet. We have compiled a list of sugar daddies from our informers and we are saying to them: "Sugar daddies, take your dirty hands off our girls!"'

There was loud applause.

'If it's right to turn a girl into a blessee, why don't you do it to your daughter?' Sibusiso continued.

The students cheered, raising their fists. Sibusiso handed the megaphone to a female student leader, Dikeledi.

'Fellow students,' said Dikeledi, 'We are organising this protest march as a follow-on to the national Women's Day we've just celebrated in August. We students of the millennium mustn't be trapped and be corrupted by the success of technology – the cellphones, laptops, Facebook and Twitter. Yes, we are living during times of democracy, but all is not well! All is not right! Women are still abused, raped and killed. Now we have this sugar daddy nonsense!'

Students applauded and cheered.

'Young girls, why are you taking your dignity and throwing it out of the window, in the name of being showered with money and gifts, by men who are old enough to be your fathers or grandfathers? This is glorified prostitution as young women are lured by older men. Blessers, you stinking old rich men! You must be ashamed to be in such an unholy business! Girls, how do you feel when you are undressing before your father? Or you don't see your father but an ATM? *Gga*! Sis! You are an embarrassment to the nation!'

Students applauded and cheered passionately.

'*Buwa sebuwi, buwaa!*' shouted a female student.

'*Buwaa!*' hollered the students.

'So today we are organising this march to say: "Enough is enough!"'

Students applauded and cheered.

'Before I sit down, let me say that as we fight this scourge of sugar daddies in our township, let us remember the girls in Mtubatuba. I have recently read in the newspapers that in that part of Kwa-Zulu Natal, blessers are making a feast in impregnating young girls. Girls of Mtubatuba, the future is in your hands. If you choose to satisfy the lust of rich old men in exchange of money and gifts, you are swallowing honey laced with poison!'

Applause broke out.

'Blessers of Mtubatuba, your days are numbered! The anti-blesser spirit that is here in Pretoria will reach your province, just like the Soweto youth revolution which spread all over South Africa and changed our country!'

Students applauded and cheered, as she handed the megaphone to another student leader, Lesiba Makgabo, the SRC secretary.

'Yes, the march is going on!' said Lesiba. 'We are going to be like the student generation of the 1970s and the 1980s who marched in the streets to defy the apartheid regime in order to change the situation. We have a list of sugar daddies in this part of Mamelodi. We are going to march to their businesses, for those who are businessmen. We'll also go to their homes! If we are forced to embarrass their wives and their children, so be it!'

Students applauded and cheered.

Sibusiso walked to Lesiba and whispered to him for a moment. Lesiba handed her the megaphone. 'We have talked a lot about the girls. What about the boys? Aren't some of them going to be tomorrow's sugar daddies and blessers? Boys, if a few years later you become rich don't be corrupted by money and think of being sugar daddies and blessers. Identify girl children and support them financially without expecting sexual favours. Treat those girls like your own daughters.'

Applause broke out.

'I have observed that all over the township there are leaflets pasted on walls and lamp posts advertising penis enlargement. In 1976 when the youth revolution in Soweto turned this country upside down, about 700 people died. Have those people sacrificed their lives so that you should think of your penises? No, guys don't be a disappointment. Forget about penis enlargement. Choose brain enlargement and help build a better South Africa!'

Another applause.

'We shall start with the business of Bigvy Masemola,' continued Lesiba. 'Our message is very clear: Hamba sugar daddy, hamba!'

'Hambaaa!' responded the students.

'Go away sugar daddy, go away!'

'Go away!!'

'Go back to your wife and children, sugar daddy, go back!'

'Go back!!'

The march was led by three student leaders standing at the back of a slow-moving bakkie. The students chanted, marched and cheered, raising their fists. Some of them waved placards. Hundreds of bystanders stood on both sides of the road cheering. Motorists, taxis and truck drivers hooted. The police in trucks, vans and sedans monitored the march. After the march had proceeded for half a kilometre the police blocked it. A police commander went to the student leaders and talked to them for a brief moment.

As the commander walked away from the bakkie, Sibusiso spoke into the megaphone: 'According to

Captain Letsoku, the police have observed that some students are collecting stones and have seen some tapping petrol from motorists. So we are told that the march cannot continue unless the culprits hand over the stones and plastic petrol containers. So please, fellow students, let's cooperate with the police.'

Sibusiso paused and at that moment about 50 students shuffled in single file to hand the stones and containers of petrol to the police waiting next to a police truck.

'Thank you for your cooperation, fellow students,' said Sibusiso. 'Permission to have the march was secured on condition that the march is peaceful, that there should be no destruction of property or injuries. The police have also advised us not to march to any business or home of those suspected to be sugar daddies. They say the situation could be explosive and lives and property could be in danger.'

18

As the students headed home Rolivhuwa went to hold a quick meeting with the student leaders to evaluate the day. An hour later as she walked briskly towards the taxi, she heard Khomisa calling from behind her.

'Are you still here, Khomi?' inquired Rolivhuwa, 'I thought you had long since left.'

Khomisa caught up with her. 'I was waiting for you, Roli.'

A navy-blue BMW with tainted windows cruised past and Rolivhuwa gazed at it until it disappeared around the street corner.

'I don't know why I have a strange feeling when I see that car,' said Rolivhuwa.

'What strange feeling?'

'That the occupants of the car are planning to do harm to me.'

'No, Roli, don't entertain that far-fetched idea. I'm going to pray for you.'

'Thank you, Khomi. I really need prayers. I thought I would have peace when I got out of the relationship with Bigvy. But I still feel something is missing. I have peace on the outside but inside life isn't okay. And I don't sleep very well, because I have nightmares that are disturbing me.

'This morning my mother told me that just before I woke up, I was shouting: "I hate you Bigvy, for using me to satisfy your lust and for infecting me with AIDS!" She said I was gnashing my teeth and clenching my fists before shouting, "To hell with you, stinking sugar daddy!"'

Khomisa put her hand on Rolivhuwa's shoulder for a brief moment. 'You definitely need God's hand to be upon you.'

'You mean that at the moment God doesn't care about me?'

'He cares about you, but He often allows your problems to bring you to Him, Roli. He uses His children as His hands and feet. God sent me to you.'

'God sent you to me? To do what?'

'To hand you an invitation.'

Rolivhuwa grinned. 'Are you serious?'

Khomisa opened her bag and took out a card which she had inserted in a book and handed it to Rolivhuwa who scrutinised it.

'But this card is from Campus Crusade for Christ,' said Rolivhuwa. 'Why do you say it's from God?'

'I've just told you that God uses people to reach others.'

Rolivhuwa studied the card. 'International Conference for Youth Leaders,' Rolivhuwa read aloud.

'Yes. Two guest speakers will be there from the US and Bahamas. They speak all over the world. The conference will be attended by actors, musicians, businessmen and politicians. So Roli, I want to urge you to attend and I can promise you, your life will never be same. The top South African gospel artists, Benjamin Dube and Solly Mahlangu will be promoting their latest CDs and DVDs.'

'And who are Beebee and Ceecee Winans?' asked Rolivhuwa pointing at the card.

'They are some of the greatest gospel artists from the US.'

'And James Okon?'

'He's one of the top gospel artists from Nigeria. I listened to his CD a few days ago; it's amazing. I haven't seen him live. He'll be coming with his band and singers. Would you like to come to me?'

Rolivhuwa looked at the floor pensively.

'Please say yes, Roli. You don't know how fortunate you are to be invited. The Campus Crusade for Christ sent only three cards per high school. So if you attend, it will be you, myself and teacher Lekota, the patron of the Students Christian Movement.

Rolivhuwa studied the card again. 'So when is it taking place?'

'Tomorrow. On Saturday.'

'Tomorrow? I'm not sure if ...'

'I'm sure there's nothing stopping you from joining me.'

'Okay, I'll attend.'

Khomisa gave Rolivhuwa a firm hug and kissed her cheeks.

* * *

When Bigvy stepped out of the silver-grey Mercedes Benz in front of his café he saw Guff waiting in his red Jeep with Kedibone. Bigvy recalled the good days when he was with Rolivhuwa. Guff walked with Bigvy to his office where they had whiskey with Coke.

'I've just seen Roli,' said Bigvy, 'you know what? Last night I dreamt about the girl; she was in my arms, and we exchanged French kisses before we made love.'

'Do your dreams often come true?'

'I wish this one could. Guff, I have slept with many girls, and I'm continuing to bed many sugar babies, but there's no girl who satisfies me better than Roli.'

Guff gulped his whiskey, contorted his face and put the glass down.

'So I'm not going to leave her alone,' continued Bigvy.

'So what are you going to do?'

'I'm going to try all the tricks in my bag to get her back into my arms. Tomorrow I'm driving to her home to see if I can speak sense into her head. I can't just get her out of my mind.'

Guff glanced at his wrist watch and rose to his feet.

'I'll see you at the fund-raising event tomorrow, Big.'

* * *

Guff and Bigvy met again during NAFCOCI'S fund-raising event at the Hyatt Hotel that Saturday evening. They were both in the company of sugar babies. They shared the same table. Bigvy's latest sugar baby was a student at Tshwane University of Technology. Hours later after serious business items had been executed and the members were enjoying drinks and music, the sugar babies went to the bathroom.

'So how was your meeting with Roli?' inquired Guff.

'I couldn't find her. I was very disappointed. Her mother told me that she left with another girl and a man driving a grey BMW.'

'Did she tell you where they had gone?'

'She said Roli just told her she would be back on Sunday.'

'You must open your eyes, Big. Someone is playing in your field.'

'I'm going to make a plan. Trust me.'

'And if you find that she's indeed in love with someone, what are you going to do? Get hit men for him?'

'I have a feeling that if I give one more push, I could get her back.'

'You are wasting your time. Just concentrate on your latest find, and forget about Roli.'

'I can't just get her out of my head. What do you suggest I do?'

Guff grinned. 'Why don't you consult those herbalists from Kenya or Tanzania, who specialise in *muti* to get lovers back and penis enlargement?'

They had a good laugh.

'I'm happy with my size,' said Bigvy as he lifted his arm and clenched fist.

They laughed again. The sugar babies returned to the table, and the men had to change the subject.

PART THREE

19

On Friday evening Rolivhuwa, Khomisa and Jack Lekota, the patron of the Students' Christian Movement, arrived at the Magaliesberg Conference Centre. They joined the queue for registrations, were given name tags and handed conference packs and then they went to their rooms. After supper the delegates went to listen to gospel music. The show started with local up-and-coming gospel artists, and gave way to the big fish, Solly Mahlangu and James Okon to end the show.

When Solly Mahlangu and his choristers sang: *Ngihamba naye*, Rolivhuwa and Khomisa stood up, together with tens of gospel lovers, snapping their fingers, gyrating and singing along, at the top of their voices: *Oh ngihamba naye, ngaphesheyaa!*

James Okon entered the stage with eight singers all dressed in the distinctly colourful Nigerian agbadas, with the women wearing matching headgear.

'Mr Lekota, what language are they singing?' Khomisa inquired.

'It's a type of English spoken in West Africa known as pidgin. He's also using, I guess, a Nigerian language, Igbo, which is spoken in the east of Nigeria.'

The audience stood and danced and sang when James Okon sang: *He's always by my side, ah very gooddooh God-doh ...*

* * *

On Saturday morning, minutes before the first part of the day started, Rolivhuwa, Khomisa and Lekota stood in front of the auditorium, in a crowd of hundreds of people, all waiting to listen to the international guest speakers, Dr Myles Munroe and Rick Warren.

Suddenly Rolivhuwa touched Khomisa's hand and pointed. 'Tell me Khomi, who's that guy? I've seen his face on TV and in newspapers!'

'He's Trevor Manuel,' said someone next to them.

'Oh,' Rolivhuwa nodded. 'And that man with a bald head?'

'He's Mr Shilowa. His wife is a businesswoman,' said the man, 'and that group of beautiful girls are actresses from popular soapies such as *Muvhango* and *Generations.*'

Dr Myles Munroe started his presentation by asking: 'What is the richest place on earth?'

Many hands shot up and enthusiastic people gave answers such as: The goldfields of Johannesburg, the platinum of Bafokeng tribe in North-West, the diamonds of Botswana and the oil-wells of Saudi Arabia.

'You got it all wrong!' said amicable Dr Munroe, 'the richest place on earth is the grave yard.'

Dr Munroe smiled and afforded his audience a moment to have what he had just told them to sink in to their heads.

'I know you are finding it hard to believe it,' continued Dr Munroe, 'I want to repeat – the richest place on earth is the grave yard, because millions have died with unfulfilled dreams: inventions, fashion, great literature, pharmaceutical drugs and unprecedented economic strategies that could rid our continent of poverty.'

The audience applauded. The title of his speech was: 'Discovering your destiny.' Rolivhuwa scribbled a lot of notes until her hand ached. A tea-break brought great relief to her painful fingers.

Rick Warren spoke about 'A Purpose-driven Life.'

'A very pertinent question that you must ask yourself this afternoon is: "What on earth am I here for?" Knowing God's purpose for creating you will reduce your stress and help you to focus your energy and simplify your decisions. This will also help to give meaning to your life.'

Rolivhuwa continued to write the notes.

'You are not an accident. Your parents may not have planned you, but God did. Your mistakes have not taken the mighty God by surprise. He will use them to confound the devil.'

Rolivhuwa filled pages and pages until her writing pad was full and she asked for more loose pages.

Rolivhuwa put her head on the pillow that night asking herself: *How is God going to use my mistakes to confound the devil?* Even in the morning as she had breakfast the same question was running through her mind.

* * *

Again, on Saturday evening local gospel artists opened the show. Benjamin Dube sang for an hour, and when his band was performing the last song, the preacher was waiting, ready with an open Bible.

'My sermon is going to be very short,' said the preacher, 'because we want you to have enough time to listen to the last part of the gospel show.'

The audience applauded.

After preaching for about 20 minutes the preacher said: 'Our Lord says, "all who are heavily burdened come to me, and I will give you rest, my yoke is easy to carry." Has the devil put a yoke on your neck? Come here in front, and we'll help you break and throw away Satan's yoke. One of our cabinet ministers once said, "We all have *smallernyana* skeletons on our cupboards. If we take them out hell will break loose!" She's partly right, but today I am inviting you to come without fear or shame, to throw out Satan's rotten skeletons, for Jesus our Lord is the boss and He's in charge here. Come! *Wa lala wa sala*!'

Rolivhuwa saw many people shuffling forward to stand in front of the preacher, and she felt an urge to go forward, but she was hesitant. Among the young women, Rolivhuwa could recognise actresses from soapies such as *Isidingo*, *Muvhango* and *Generations*. Rolivhuwa said to herself: *If these celebrities whom I adore so much need God, who am I to say no!* So she stood up and joined them.

Tears meandered down Rolivhuwa's cheeks. A woman counsellor standing in the aisle went over to her.

'Have you any problem? Can I help you?'

'Yes, ma'am,' Rolivhuwa continued to sob. 'I'm angry with my mother for insisting that I should continue with my relationship with a sugar daddy; and I'm also angry with that stinking old guy for infecting me with AIDS. In fact, I'm bitter! I feel used and cheap, and I'm considering suicide. I hate myself for what I did ...'

'No, my girl,' said a smiling counsellor, 'In God's eyes you are a fresh untouched virgin. If you confess your sins, He allows you to start afresh. He says though your sins are as red as scarlet, I will wipe them off.'

The counsellor paused and smiled: 'Any question?'

'No, ma'am,' said Rolivhuwa.

'Are you now ready to receive Jesus as Lord and Saviour?'

'Yes ma'am.'

'Let's go to the pastor.'

When Rolivhuwa returned from the pastor, where she had been guided to receive Jesus, she found Beebee and Ceecee Winans, the main gospel attraction form the US, on stage; the audience was standing, dancing and singing along.

20

At Solomon Mahlangu High that Monday during break, Rolivhuwa was in the company of Khomisa and other girls who were members of the SCM. A group of girls standing metres away enjoying *sphatlo* and juices pointed towards Rolivhuwa.

'She has become a *mzalwane*,' said one of the girls.

She saw Kedibone from a distance and waved at her. When Kedibone folded her arms and turned away with a scowl, Rolivhuwa responded with a grin.

After school, as Rolivhuwa walked towards the gate, two girls stopped her. 'What happened with you, Roli?' asked one of the girls. 'You have a huge smile as if you've won the lotto.'

Rolivhuwa chortled. 'Thanks for the compliment, Thoko. I just feel light; I have energy and I just feel like running.'

'Really?' inquired another girl.

'Yes, I feel as if a huge load which was weighing me down has suddenly fallen away.'

The girls exchanged glances. 'So no more sugar daddies?' asked Thoko.

'Yes, of course! And if any sugar daddy says "Hallo babes!" I'm going to smile and reply: "You need Jesus to spice up your life."'

'Amen *mamfundisi*, amen!' said one girl.

'Amen!' the other chorused.

The girls laughed aloud.

* * *

On Sunday Khomisa picked up Rolivhuwa and they took a taxi to the House of Glory Church. As they entered the church the band, comprising a keyboard player, lead guitarist, bass guitarist and a conga drummer, was already playing, and four vocalists were singing. Rolivhuwa sat beside Khomisa and observed what was going on: the parishioners were standing, singing an upbeat chorus, clapping their hands and swaying a little to the right and left.

During the second song Khomisa bowed and spoke to Rolivhuwa. 'You can stand and enjoy yourself.'

Rolivhuwa hesitated; Khomisa smiled at her and grabbed her by her hand. 'Com'n Roli,' insisted Khomisa who gradually pulled Rolivhuwa up onto her feet.

Rolivhuwa chuckled and immediately became part of the scores of worshipers having fun in church. Khomisa took out a book-mark on which the words of a song, 'God's week', were printed and handed it to

Rolivhuwa who had to learn the new song:

'*Without God our week would be: Mournday, Tearsday, Wasteday, Thirstday, Fightday, Shatterday and Sinday. But with God, Monday, Tuesday, Wednesday, Thursday, Friday, Saturday and Sunday are good days.*'

Thirty minutes later Pastor Titus Sithole walked to the podium. 'Those who are visiting our church for the first time,' said Pastor Titus, 'please stand up!'

Rolivhuwa was one of ten people who were enthusiastically welcomed with loud applause, whistles and drum-beats.

'Welcome to the family of God!' said the pastor.

People on the left and right of Rolivhuwa gave her firm handshakes.

After the service, Rolivhuwa and nine others were invited to a huge lounge at the administration block, where they were served tea and sandwiches. They were each given a Bible. They were told that if they were interested in being members of the church they should attend orientation regarding church membership for the next four weeks.

At the end of the welcoming session, Rolivhuwa walked to Khomisa who was waiting at the car park. As they walked to the taxi pick-up area Rolivhuwa flipped over the Good News translation Bible, and she found an envelope with the words *a little gift* written on the front. Rolivhuwa excitedly showed Khomisa the envelope.

Khomisa radiated a huge smile. 'Well, God has answered your prayer!'

Rolivhuwa laughed.

'Last week,' said Khomisa, 'a young woman who used to be a prostitute was given money to start a hair salon.'

'That's wonderful,' said Rolivhuwa who opened her envelope and found R2000.

'It's good that you have been given money,' said Khomisa, 'so that no sugar daddy should tempt you.'

Rolivhuwa smiled, looked at the bank notes and gave Khomisa a bear hug and a kiss.

'Now you should take R200 and give it to the church,' said Khomisa, 'that is called a tithe or a tenth of what you have been given or earned.'

They walked and stood next to the taxi area. A white Audi with tinted windows drove past.

'I don't know why I feel so uncomfortable when I see that car,' said Rolivhuwa.

'Why?'

'I just feel that the occupants of the car are planning some harm to me ... I have a feeling that they may abduct me.'

'Abduct you?' asked Khomisa, 'No, Roli stop being negative! You are now a Christian, so you must believe in God's goodness. Don't be like Job who said: "The thing which I greatly fear comes upon me."'

Khomisa touched Rolivhuwa's shoulder. 'You are a new convert; I understand, so we are going to pray for you.'

'Thank you, Khomi.'

21

Late on Sunday afternoon Bigvy visited Rolivhuwa.

'Roli, my apple-tart, I've paid you a visit,' said Bigvy, jingling the car keys, 'In fact I want to take you out for a delicious lunch.'

'I won't accept your invitation, Mr Masemola.'

'You know, babes, I just can't get you out of my mind. Day and night. If you agree to renew our relationship, I'll take you to Mauritius, the island of …'

'I'm not interested, Mr Masemola.'

'Why?'

'I'm now …'

'Sh!' Bigvy tried to place his forefinger on her lips, but she bent her neck backward.

'Before you answer me. Let me tell you something, honey.'

'I'm not going to accept the devil's poison laced with honey. I'm now a Christian. Light can't keep company with darkness.'

'You call me darkness?'

'That's what my Bible is telling me. Perhaps I'm rude to you. I'm sorry.'

'Anyway, if you are Christian, it's fine with me. I can take you to church, and pick you up from there, as long as you are my ...'

'That's impossible Mr Masemola. Let me repeat: I'm now a Christian. And I want to advise any sugar daddy, "Please don't follow me, follow Jesus!"'

'Come on Roli, stop preaching to me. I'm not against you going to church. Look here!'

Bigvy took out his purse, pinched out some notes and put them in front of Rolivhuwa. 'It's your pocket money!' said Bigvy grinning.

Rolivhuwa shook her head. 'No, I won't take it, Mr Masemola. The church has just given me some cash.'

Bigvy grinned. 'Is the pastor your new sugar D?'

'Oh no please Mr Masemola, don't speak ...'

'Okay, how much?'

'None of your business!'

'Tell me because I want to double that amount. And the church isn't going to buy you a car when you pass Grade 12. It's only Bigvy who can do that. If you cooperate, I'm going to buy you a red Porsche Boxter, and you ...'

'I would rather walk on foot than accept a sugar daddy's gift. That's poison mixed with honey!'

Again Bigvy took out his purse, pulled out several R200 notes and added them to the money that was in front of Rolivhuwa. 'It's now three grand. It's far more than your church's money! Bless you!' said Bigvy, smiling.

'I don't need any of your rotten promises, Mr Masemola. And take that money to an orphanage, or an old age home,' said Rolivhuwa, 'I don't need it.'

Bigvy stood and left the money in front of Rolivhuwa and walked out of the house.

'Take this money, Mr Masemola, or else I'm going to ask my cousin to take it to your wife!'

Bigvy returned, took the money and hurried out of the house in a huff. Rolivhuwa's mother entered the lounge where her daughter was standing, looking at Bigvy's car driving away.

Rolivhuwa waved. 'Bye bye Mr Masemola. Hamba Sugar D!'

'Vhovho, why aren't you accepting the money?' queried Rolivhuwa's mother.

'I don't want it.'

'You should have given it to me.'

'Well go and ask for it from Mr Masemola.'

'You've done a foolish thing, Vhovho.'

'I've done a wise thing, in God's eyes, Mama.'

'You have angered Mr Masemola, and he's going to take away the furniture.'

'Let him take it! God is going to restore what the devil has taken away!'

Rolivhuwa heaved a sigh as her mother looked at her with confusion and disappointment. 'Mama, you should be proud of the step I have taken. I'm not going back to the cage I have been saved from. Mama, do you still remember what Aunt Bertha said during my birthday party?'

'I don't remember. How can I remember? That one talks to us like she's a social worker.'

'Okay, let me remind you. She said you as an adult should be giving me sound advice instead of behaving like a cheerleader. And according to my Bible ...'

Her mother blocked her ears. 'Okay, I'm not going to listen to your sermon! Oh Jehovah of peace, help my daughter to come to her senses, Amen!'

* * *

A week later Bigvy called Guff.

'Any progress?' asked Guff.

'None. I've paid a lost-love muti-man R2000. I was first impressed when he sprinkled her photo with water mixed with herbs, swearing she would return within 48 hours. That hasn't happened. What a waste!'

'So what are you going to do? Give up?'

'No ways! You'll see what I'm going to do.'

'Talk is cheap. According to the Bapedi tribespeople, "A mouth crosses a river in floods."'

'You wait and see!'

22

Rolivhuwa woke up early, intending to sit alone in the classroom and do revision for her final examinations. Her mother had just awoken when she left the yard, the gate creaking as she closed it. She had braided her hair and was in her school uniform. She walked down the street singing James Okon's gospel song: *He's always by my side*. Before she arrived at a T-junction a red BMW slowed down and stopped; she was walking on the left side of the road; a man in the passenger's seat smiled at her.

'Sorry baby,' said the man, wearing a red golf cap. 'Can I ask for a direction to this high school …?'

The man paused as he took a piece of paper from his shirt pocket. Rolivhuwa responded with a bright smile and stepped towards the passenger. She had quickly assessed the car and the occupants; if the car was a white Audi or a navy blue BMW, she would have walked away.

The man showed her a piece of paper. 'It's the name of this school. I can't pronounce it. So can you please help?'

At that moment a passenger in the back seat stepped out of the car speaking on his cellphone.

As Rolivhuwa was looking at the piece of paper, the man who was speaking on his cellphone suddenly turned around towards her, armed with a gun, which he placed against her left ribs.

'Shh! You make any noise, I shoot you!' he said, pushing the gun very hard into her side. 'Bitch, get into the car!'

The man pushed her into the car where she found another armed man. The driver revved the engine which began to 'eat up' kilometres, heading towards the Cullinan road. A man on her left proffered an open palm. 'Give me your cellphone, and don't play games, okay?'

Rolivhuwa took out her cellphone and handed it to the man. A cellphone rang and the man in the passenger's seat answered it.

'We caught the bird, boss ... yes, boss ... we are going to do that in a minute.'

A man sitting on her right took a woman's sun-hat and put it on her head and tilted it forward to hide a part of her face. Rolivhuwa's heart was hammering in her rib-cage; she bowed her head and sobbed until her shoulders quivered.

'Shut up, *sefebe*,' shouted a man on her left. 'We knew we would catch the dove.'

The man on her right rubbed her thighs and grinned. 'Very soon someone is going to enjoy what's between these fresh thighs. Delicious Christian cake!'

The car left the main road and veered into dense bush; the moment the car stopped she was blindfolded with a thick piece of a black cloth.

23

At Rolivhuwa's school the teacher inquired about her but no one knew where she was. During break Khomisa expected to see her. When Khomisa was told that Rolivhuwa was absent she went to the teacher.

'Ma'am Serakalala,' said Khomisa, 'I'm very concerned that Roli is absent today, and I don't want us to wait until tomorrow. Can you please send someone to her home to find out why she's absent?'

'Have you tried to call her?' inquired Ms Serakalala.

'Yes Ma'am, her phone goes straight to voicemail. Something might have gone seriously wrong.'

'Why do you think that?'

'On two occasions she observed cars that made her a little uncomfortable. At one time she said she feared that she might be abducted.'

Khomisa and Serakalala drove to Rolivhuwa's home where her mother told them that she had gone to school. From there Rolivhuwa's mother drove with them to the police station where a docket of suspected abduction was opened. They dropped Rolivhuwa's mother at her house and drove to school.

After school, Khomisa asked the Students' Christian Movement members to remain. She told them what happened to Rolivhuwa.

'So brethren,' said Khomisa, 'we have to pray and fast for Roli's safety.' They joined hands and prayed aloud. Someone knocked on the door as they were praying.

'What are you doing here when the students are holding an emergency meeting?' asked a male student, who was not a member of the SRC, who normally held student meetings.

The student asked them to accompany him to the auditorium, and quickly updated them. The purpose of the meeting was to organise a march to the police station.

'The convenors aren't the SRC, but the Friends of Roli,' said the student.

Khomisa and her associates sat down and listened to the leader speaking.

'Are the placards ready?' asked the leader.

'Yes!' shouted a student who raised a placard written: 'Why Bigvy?'

Another placard was inscribed: 'Bigvy Suspect No 1.'

'We shall take Mangaliso Sobukwe Avenue and turn into FF Ribeiro Street, straight to the police station. There we are going to demand the immediate arrest of Bigvy Masemola.'

A student raised his hand. 'What are we going to do if the police delay arresting Mr Masemola?'

'If Mr Masemola isn't arrested within 24 hours we shall march to the police station, carrying stones and plastic containers filled with petrol.'

The students applauded.

At the police station the students were told by the station commander that as a result of an anonymous telephone call, Bigvy had already been interrogated and was released with a warning that he should not influence or intimidate those he could perceive as possible witnesses against him.

* * *

From the police station Khomisa went to inform the church leadership about Rolivhuwa's disappearance. As a result, three vigils were held, two at the church on Friday and Saturday, and one at Rolivhuwa's home on Sunday. On Sunday evening before midnight the women of the church were singing a hymn when they heard a knock at the door. A woman opened it and found a policeman and a policewoman standing outside.

'Is this the home of Rolivhuwa Ramabulana?' inquired the policewoman.

'Yes,' responded Rolivhuwa's mother, after evaluating the officers, 'have you good or bad news?'

'Let's tell you what we are here for,' said the

policeman. 'You'll decide if it's good or bad. How are you related to her?'

'I'm her mother.'

'Your daughter was dropped at the police station by a man unknown to her,' said the policewoman, 'she told us what happened to her. Because she was traumatised and exhausted we drove her to the hospital. She gave us this address.'

'Praise the Lord, hallelujah!' said one of the women emotionally.

'Amen!' said the other women.

The officers handed Rolivhuwa's mother the telephone number for the hospital and left the house. Rolivhuwa's mother called the hospital and she was told that Rolivhuwa could be visited only during visiting time on Monday at 3pm.

24

Rolivhuwa was resting her head against the headboard of the hospital bed, looking at people who mattered in her life: her mother, Khomisa, her aunt, the pastor and his wife and two church elders. All earnestly wanted to know what happened to her between Friday morning and Sunday evening.

'I was blindfolded for over an hour, and I had no idea of the direction. When the blindfold was removed I found myself in a plot full of many tall trees. My two captors wore balaclavas.

'The other two men and the car were nowhere to be seen. I heard the car driving away while I was still blindfolded. We were facing a mansion that had a parking garage for four cars. I was taken to a chalet where I was given a glass of water. The chalet had a lounge and a bedroom and the windows had burglar bars, and armed guards stood outside holding walky-talkies.

'So any hope of escape quickly vanished. I was given salads, fried chicken, rice and cooked vegetables and a litre of fruit juice. I was hungry so I ate all the food and drank half of the juice. I was given a women's magazine, which I could not read. The book I wanted was the Bible. I also had a TV. I was told to have a bath and I was given pyjamas and a night gown.

'At dusk the two men, still covering their faces, entered the chalet and sat in front of me.

'Man A, said: "Roli, I'm sure you can see that we aren't bad guys," he spoke pleasantly. Even if I couldn't see his face, I had a feeling that he was smiling.

'Man B said: "Yes, we've abducted you, but we are still good guys. How long you'll be kept here depends on you."

'I said: "Who are you?" and one of them said: "None of your business." I put the question differently and asked: "Who sent you? Was it Bigvy?"

'Man A replied: "None of your business!"

'Man B said: "Roli, we don't want to harm you; you know what you have done; if you can change your mind you'll be released." I replied him: "I'm not going to change my mind!"

'Man A gestured towards Man B and they stood up.

'Man A said: "See you tomorrow, good night!"

Before they left the chalet Man B turned towards me and said: "We hope you'll cooperate tomorrow."

'I watched TV until after midnight, hoping that I would become drowsy, but I only fell asleep at 2am.

'On Saturday during the day and night, and on Sunday during the day, they were nice to me, giving me food and drinks. Their message was the same: "If you change your mind, we shall release you."

'One of them became very straightforward and said: "Why don't you reconcile with Bigvy because he has been so nice to you?" The other man went on: "And you can go to the police and tell them that you had not been abducted but that you were on holiday."

'I replied: "I'm not going to change my mind. If I go back to Mr Masemola I will be like a dog returning to its vomit." I also said: "I'm not prepared to lie that I was on holiday."

'On Sunday evening they blindfolded me. Man A said: "Roli, you have freedom of choice. You have chosen to keep yourself longer." Man B said: "So what's going to happen to you is the result of what you've chosen."

'They blindfolded me, stripped me naked, covered me with a night gown and led me to another room where they made me sit on the bed.

'Man A said: 'Roli, this is your last chance to change your mind."

'"What are you saying?" I said: "I told you I won't change my mind!"

'I was told to stand up, and I felt a man removing the night gown and start to kiss me and to fondle my breasts and touch me all over my body and brush my thighs. One of the men instructed me to lie down facing the ceiling. I felt one of them touching my pubic area, opening my thighs and lie on me. From his weight and smell I could feel that he was Bigvy. When he tried to put his penis into me, I screamed and prayed: "God please protect me! Fire of the Holy Spirit, please cover me!"

'Suddenly the man dismounted. I heard the men whispering, and I felt Bigvy lying on me again, trying to penetrate me. I shouted: "God please protect me!" And I felt someone slap my cheek saying: "Bitch, shut up! If you open your mouth again, your life will be in danger!"

'For the third time Bigvy tried to rape me, and I prayed in my heart. Again Bigvy dismounted me, and said, "This bitch is a witch!" I further heard the men whispering. One man said: "Stand up!" I felt a man pulling me upward and I was led to another room where they removed the blindfold; I saw the two men who had covered their faces. They told me to put on my school uniform and take my schoolbag.

'They held me by both arms and walked me to the car and I sat between them on the back seat; the car was idling. When the car started driving away, they blindfolded me. After about two hours the car stopped and they took me out of the car, removed the cloth from my eyes, left me by the roadside and drove away.

'I guessed from the street lights that I was outside Mamelodi. A car came and I stopped it; I was relieved when I found a man and his wife in the car. I told them briefly what had happened to me and asked them to take me to the police station. My people, don't cry or feel bad about what happened to me. Thank God that

He protected me. Bigvy tried to rape me. But his penis dropped dead. God caused his thing to be weak like wool.'

'Hallelujah!' shouted the pastor's wife.

'Amen!' the church leaders agreed.

25

That Monday morning Rolivhuwa woke up at half past three. By five she had bathed, had breakfast and was in her school uniform. After reading her pocket Bible she paged through her note books, trying to recall the last lessons. When she went to bid her mother goodbye, she asked her to wait.

'Vhovo, do you feel safe? Let me accompany you.'

'Please don't stress, Mama. God's angels are my bodyguards.'

'God's angels are your bodyguards? Where were they when you were abducted on Friday?'

'They were there.'

'They were there? So why didn't they stop …?'

'Let's not ask too many whys, Mama. God knows why this has happened. What's important is the fact that I am still alive.'

Her mother shrugged as Rolivhuwa closed the door behind her with a smile.

Rolivhuwa arrived at school so early that she had to wait for the night watchman to open her classroom. When her class mates entered the classroom and saw her they rushed to her desk, overjoyed and gave her hugs. Suddenly the message was spread at all classrooms, 'She's back! She's back!'

Ms Legodi was the first teacher to be informed. She hastened to the classroom and gave Rolivhuwa hugs and kisses before she took her to the staff room via the principal's office. The headmaster and staff joked that the school should get her bodyguards.

'I'm sorry about what happened to you, Roli,' said mma-Legodi, who had taken Rolivhuwa to her cubicle.

'It's okay Ma'am, there's a good reason why this happened to me.'

'You are right, Roli. You know, yesterday I listened to an interesting programme on Radio Pulpit.'

'Radio what?'

'Radio Pulpit. It's a Christian radio station. The presenter is a well-known counsellor, and she encourages listeners going through difficult times. She said, "When life hands you lemons don't cry, *Joo, mma-wee,* life is unfair! Why should I suck bitter lemons? No, don't be miserable but smile, take the lemons and make some fresh lemonade!"'

'Oh, what an encouraging statement!' Rolivhuwa took a notebook and a pen and started to scribble. 'Can you repeat it, Ma'am?'

'I have asked the station to send me an audio tape. So, you can listen to the tape as many times as you like and write notes. The title of the tape is 'Turning lemons into lemonade'. Listen to what she also mentioned: "When life throws bricks at you, don't cry, *Joo, mma-wee!* Why me! Why have I bad-luck? No, don't be miserable but smile, take the bricks and use them as stairs on the journey towards your dream."'

'That's fantastic! You are really a blessing Ma'am!'

They exchanged a hug.

Mma-Legodi smiled at her. 'Now let's talk about your dream. You said you want to be a CA?'

'Yes, Ma'am.'

'First, your dream should be so big that it consumes you, and you talk about it all the time. If you announce your dream, it energises you.'

Rolivhuwa took out her notebook and wrote the advice down.

'Secondly, you must write down your dream.'

Rolivhuwa continued to jot down some notes.

'If you write down your dream … Okay Roli, stop writing.' Rolivhuwa looked at mma-Legodi who handed her a book.

'Please read aloud all what I have highlighted in the book.'

Rolivhuwa took the book and read: 'If you write down your dream, it conditions your behaviour.'

She read further down the page: 'Announcement of your dream makes it difficult for you to fail. It attracts support and resources.' Rolivhuwa paused and scrutinised the cover of the book and saw the photo of a bespectacled man wearing a black suit, a white shirt and a tie. She read the title: *Advance Your Life: Practical Advice You Need to Succeed* by Dr John Tibane.

'Where did you buy this book, Ma'am?'

'I bought it directly from the writer – I heard him speaking on radio and I placed an order.'

'Can you lend me the book?'

'You can have it. I decided to bless you!'

'Ooh, Ma'am, thank you very much!' Rolivhuwa hugged and kissed her.

26

Time moved very fast for Rolivhuwa because she was expending her energy not only in her studies, but in drama, church youth activities and home chores. Late at night before she slept, she often self-directed her part in the script – late at night when she was alone, just before she slept. At school during break she went to rehearse with the cast. One day as she was coming back from the rehearsals Khomisa said to her, 'How's life? Hectic?'

'Yes very hectic, Khomi!' responded Rolivhuwa. 'The way I'm busy, the devil has no chance.'

They laughed, only to realise quickly that Kedibone was looking at them from a distance with utter displeasure.

Very soon it was time to perform *Hamba Sugar Daddy!* at the auditorium of the Mamelodi campus of the University of Pretoria. Grade 11 and 12 students from high schools all over Mamelodi had been brought to the venue. The headmasters and some teachers also attended. The Gauteng MEC for Education had been invited.

Two hours before the play started the performers were rehearsing under the watchful eye of the director. The Drama Department of Tshwane University of Technology had sent their drama students to do practical training; so they helped in directing, costumes, make-up, stage building and lighting.

At the right time the lights were switched off. The spot light was on Rolivhuwa who entered, commanding an impressive stage presence, in the role of the main character.

'My name is Siphokazi Mabena from D5 in Mamelodi West,' Rolivhuwa delivered her opening line. 'Can I tell you how I became a rich man's sugar baby? My parents are unemployed and are receiving a grant. So when this man, *ntate* Mavundla, started to come to my home with nice things, he easily won their hearts and he had them in his pockets. I could see that they started to enjoy a new good life.'

As the sketch progressed, Rolivhuwa saw the MEC nodding and smiling; so she was encouraged. In the next scene, Rolivhuwa as Siphokazi entered the stage blocking her ears, while a performer acting as her mother was waving a forefinger.

'I say listen to me, Siphokazi,' shouted her 'mother', 'I told you that you can't leave *ntate* Mavundla because he's going to take the furniture and demand back the money he has been giving you!'

'Let him take them, let him take them! I'm tired of being his sex slave! He looks like a toad, and I have to shut my eyes whenever I have sex with him. I hate him! Because you don't want him to go away, I have organised my male cousins; so, when he comes here together we are going to say: "Hamba sugar daddy, you ugly toad!"'

There was loud applause.

At the end of the sketch, as the performers had joined and bowed, the students rose to their feet, shouting: 'We want more! We want more!'

A member of the principals' forum stood and introduced the MEC.

'I'm highly impressed with what I've seen here in Mamelodi today,' said the MEC. 'I have no doubt that these young students are doing an excellent task in unearthing promising talent. The drama is taking place at the right time when the Gauteng Department of Education and the Department of Health, are planning a campaign against sugar daddies in December. We are following the footsteps of KwaZulu-Natal's Ministry of Health whose research findings have revealed that a large number of young girls have become carriers of HIV/AIDS by dating older men who are well off.

'While the marketing concept to be communicated has been planned, what you have presented in this sketch is going to complement it. Your well-performed play is driving the message home, and the beautiful thing about your drama is that it is being presented by students who are talking to their peers in the way they'll understand best. I can promise you that I'm going to recommend to the provincial cabinet that we should sponsor your sketch.'

There was loud applause.

After handing the special certificates of participation to the performers, the MEC said: 'I also have the best performer's award. Who should get it?'

'Roli, Roli, Roli,' shouted the students with one voice.

Rolivhuwa felt a few centimetres taller as she was awarded a golden trophy. She lifted it upwards, kissed it and waved it, as the students applauded.

27

For days Rolivhuwa basked in the glory of being the award-winning actress in *Hamba Sugar Daddy*. Cherishing the message in the book of Ecclesiastes that there is a season for everything, she interpreted one of the verses to be addressing her specific situation: 'Time to prepare for the examinations, and time to write and pass the examinations.' So, she decided to focus her time and energy on studying. Mma-Legodi was fond of saying to the Grade 12 learners, 'Matric is not a mattress.' She also added in Sepedi, 'Sleep does not buy a cow.' And she continued in English. 'Matric will open doors of many careers and therefore many job opportunities. So, if you want to pass Grade 12, you've got to work very hard, boys and girls.'

Rolivhuwa had in her spare time read Dr Tibane's motivational book: *Advance Your Life: Practical Advice You Need to Succeed*. She had written out the key points which she had pasted on the wall in her bedroom where she studied.

Months ago she had applied to study for a BCom Accounting degree at the University of Cape Town. One day her mother saw a white envelope with the logo and the letters 'UCT' addressed to her and she read the letter.

'R40 000 for accommodation and R30 000 for tuition!' her mother said with an icy tone, 'Vhovho, how are you going to pay this huge amount? Will your church or pastor help? Mh? If you had not parted with Mr Masemola he would ...'

'Mama, please stop talking about Mr Masemola! It's no use crying over spilt milk. God will provide for my studies.'

Her mother grinned bitterly. 'We shall see by the stripes that indeed they are zebras!'

'Members of the church are praying for me. And I believe that my God will not disappoint me.'

Her mother shrugged and shuffled off to prepare her afternoon tea.

Rolivhuwa belonged to a study group which comprised five learners, including Khomisa. They began and ended their studies with a short prayer. A day before they wrote the first paper in English Khomisa said a word of encouragement to them, 'Remember Pastor Chris Oyakhilhome's advice that we aren't ordinary but extra-ordinary learners because we have Daniel's excellent spirit.'

* * *

During the first weekend after writing the last paper Rolivhuwa and Khomisa went to the Denlyn shopping mall at the western entrance of Mamelodi to distribute gospel leaflets. They handed the leaflets to shoppers going into and out of the mall. They also inserted some between the wipers and the windshields of parked cars. A policewoman passing by looked on with curiosity for a moment and then went to read the headline on the leaflet.

'Why does this say "Hijacked"? Don't you think it's going to scare the car owner who will think that it has to do with a real hijacking?'

Rolivhuwa stepped towards the policewoman armed with a smile. 'It's a gospel leaflet, officer. It's just a way to catch the reader's attention – with a sort of a shocker.'

'Let me read one or two sentences,' Khomisa chipped in. '"This modern age has produced a new drama – Hijacking! One boards a plane to California and lands in Cuba. Most of us will probably never experience what it is like when somebody holding a hand grenade takes control of an aeroplane ... The greatest and most dangerous hijacker of all time is Satan ..."'

The officer responded with a grin and a nod before she left them.

* * *

The following weekend Rolivhuwa and Khomisa continued to distribute leaflets when young women wearing the yellow T-shirts and blue caps of Mamelodi Sundowns Football Club distributed their leaflets.

'You are invited to join us next weekend at Moretele Park as we celebrate the success of our team,' said the first young woman as she handed Rolivhuwa the leaflet.

'Remember that *Bafana ba* Style has walloped Kaizer Chief 3–0!' said the second young woman.

Rolivhuwa glanced at an A5 leaflet showing a photo of the team wearing yellow jerseys and blue pants lifting up a huge silver trophy, spreading their arms and showing their teeth – shouting triumphantly. The goal-keeper Denis Onyango and the head coach Pitso Mosimane were in the middle of the second row. She read the caption below the colour photo: '*Hola Masandawana.* The sky is the limit!' Below the caption she continued to read, 'Congratulations to Mamelodi Sundowns on winning the Absa Premiership season.'

Rolivhuwa studied the photo.

'Their ecstasy is infectious,' said Khomisa.

'Yes. And I like the slogan, *The sky is the limit!*' said Rolivhuwa. 'It's an excellent motivational statement!'

'Yes. Let's attend the occasion, Roli. I have a feeling that we could get important contacts.'

'Yes. I want to take a selfie with Mr Motsepe, the club owner.'

'Me too!'

28

Rolivhuwa and Khomisa arrived an hour before the celebration began at Moretele Park. As Khomisa had suggested they volunteered to help the catering team. They approached a long row of catering tables joined together with green and yellow cloths. As they walked past the stage they saw some technicians busy with a sound check. Rolivhuwa read the slogan, *The sky is the limit!* written in green letters on a yellow background at the back of the stage.

'This slogan is speaking to me, Khomi,' said Rolivhuwa, 'Before I put my head on the pillow last night and just after I had woken up, I've been telling myself, *The sky is your limit*, Roli!'

They introduced themselves to the manager of the catering team and begged him to squeeze them into the group of volunteers. He took them to the supervisor who gladly welcomed them and showed them what needed to be done to help in packing the lunch boxes comprising rice, chicken, mashed potato, tomato gravy and mixed vegetables wrapped separately. They also added a banana, an apple and a tinned cold drink.

An hour later, as people entered the park, local up-and-coming bands entertained the club's thousands of supporters wearing yellow T-shirts, caps and helmets known as *makarapa*. It took two hours to serve the supporters who filed up in several snaking queues. Khomisa and Rolivhuwa at last found a moment to sit down, have their meals and chat with other members of the catering team.

When they inquired about the supporters' membership they were introduced to the marketing officer, Mpho Maleka, who showed them a table where they filled in the application forms. Mpho, eager to know more about them, told them that the club's president was going to make an important announcement. He also asked them if they would be volunteers to help in the fast-growing supporters' coordinator desk. When they indicated their enthusiasm he took their cell numbers.

At last the club's owner, President Patrice Motsepe, stood up as loud applause thundered all across the park. He started by thanking the supporters for consistently lending enthusiastic support to the team even during drought years when the players were not winning, the troubled times when some fans vociferously wanted him to fire the head coach.

'Thank you for your patience and understanding when I appealed to you to be more considerate,' said Mr Motsepe.

The audience applauded uproariously.

He also told the supporters about how he still

wanted to shop around for good players all over the world, particularly Latin America.

He then made the announcement Rolivhuwa and Khomisa were waiting for: 'You are all aware of the Motsepe Foundation's funding programme for welfare projects of various communities countrywide. We have also decided to offer bursaries to deserving students of this community to study at tertiary institutions. Offering ...'

Loud applause interrupted him.

'Offering bursaries is the best way of uplifting communities and breaking the cycle of poverty. So, those of you who have passed Grade 12 can get forms at our Pretoria offices at Church Square without delay.'

As the audience clapped their hands, Rolivhuwa and Khomisa high-fived and laughed aloud. Mr Motsepe took his seat in the midst of applause, cheers and whistles.

* * *

During the new week Rolivhuwa and Khomisa collected, completed and submitted the bursary applications forms.

A week later, which was the second week of December, Rolivhuwa received a call from Mpho who invited them to the first supporters' coordinator's meeting, to be held at a restaurant in Menlyn shopping centre in Pretoria. At the end of the meeting Rolivhuwa and Khomisa were assigned the task of answering cellphone calls, the registrations of forms online and sending out SMSs.

At the end of the meeting Mpho called Rolivhuwa and Khomisa aside and offered them a lift. After dropping the club's secretary Mpho asked Rolivhuwa to sit on the passenger's seat beside him. Rolivhuwa and Khomisa were the only passengers.

'I don't want to feel like a chauffeur delivering VIPs,' Mpho joked, evoking loud peals of laughter from them.

Minutes later Khomisa bid them goodbye and alighted. As he drove slowly to her home Rolivhuwa saw his smile which she felt was reserved for her, but she dismissed the thought.

'What are you doing during this weekend?' Mpho asked.

'Nothing in particular, except helping with the usual chores.'

'Will you join me for the Pretoria derby on Saturday at Loftus Versfeld stadium? Sundowns will be playing against Supersport United. I want you to sit with me in the executive suite.'

'Thank you so much, *abuti* Mpho!'

'It's a pleasure to be a blessing to other people.'

'Thank you, *abuti* Mpho. Whenever the camera showed us the VIPs on the executive suite, I always wished I could one day sit there.'

'Well today your prayer has been answered.'

* * *

As Mpho led her to their seats she looked around and recognised the faces of several famous people, including the Minister of Sport and celebrities sitting all over the suite. Minutes before the match started he quickly organised something to eat and drink. Once the whistle was blown Mpho concentrated with mounting tension as their opponent repeatedly threatened to pierce through the defence wall in quest of a goal. But luck smiled on Sundowns when, a minute before half-time, Hlompho Kekana unleashed an unstoppable fiery shot. In sheer excitement Mpho raised his palms, high-fived with Rolivhuwa, hugged her and slapped her back as if she were the goal-scorer.

* * *

That Friday Rolivhuwa and Khomisa were completing a week as volunteers stationed at the Denlyn shopping centre. During lunch Mpho, who worked at the head office at Chloorkop in Midrand, entered the office carrying six lunch-packs and invited all the staff to come and help themselves. He left thirty minutes later, explaining that he was rushing to a meeting at the municipal offices.

'*Abuti* Mpho is a nice guy, but not to an extent that he can buy anyone a lunch-pack,' said one of the girls called Grace. 'I suspect he's doing this because of you girls.' She was gesturing towards Rolivhuwa and Khomisa. 'What makes you special?'

Rolivhuwa laughed. 'I don't think we are special.'

'You are. There's something fishy. Or perhaps I should say there's something *rosy* going on?'

Khomisa laughed while Rolivhuwa shrugged with a grin.

* * *

'I think Grace is right. *Abuti* Mpho is a nice guy,' said Khomisa as they walked to the taxi pick-up area.

'I think he likes us. What do you think?' said Rolivhuwa.

'*Abuti* Mpho likes *you*, Roli.'

Rolivhuwa chortled. 'Ooh, what makes you think so?'

'It's the way he looks and smiles at you.'

Rolivhuwa continued to laugh aloud. 'You are really exaggerating, my friend. We all like *abuti* Mpho and we smile at him as our boss, don't we?'

Deep in her heart Rolivhuwa agreed Khomisa, but chose to ignore an emotional elephant in the room. Rolivhuwa had not told Khomisa that Mpho had taken her out. She had said to herself, *Let me not be too hasty to disclose my wishes and fantasies and be disappointed soon when it happens to be just a passing fancy of a romantic guy.*

29

During the first Friday of the new year Rolivhuwa and Khomisa went to the Department of Education to check the Grade 12 examination results. It was a re-union of some kind with everybody wanting to know who had passed what, who could not make it, who was going to which tertiary institution. Rolivhuwa and Khomisa returned from the huge notice-board laughing aloud, after high-fiving, kissing and hugging. They also wiped away tears of joy. They had both got three distinctions: Rolivhuwa's distinctions were in accounting, business economics and mercantile law.

That afternoon when she arrived home and had shared the good news, she found a yellow envelope in their letter box. Her heart beat a little faster when she realised it was from the Motsepe Foundation.

Dear Miss R. Ramabulana

I am pleased to inform you that your application for a bursary to study for a B.Com Accounting degree has been successful. You have been offered a bursary for four years, renewable annually depending on your results. Please report to our Pretoria offices ASAP.

Regards,
(signed)
PP Pookgwadi

'Mama! Mama! I got a bursary for four years!' said Rolivhuwa as she hastened to her mother at the sink. 'I told you that God will provide. I'm going to UCT!'

'Hallelujah!' her mother exclaimed, surprising herself and her daughter for that unusual manner of appreciation. 'Well done, my child! Indeed God has provided as you said.' Her mother hugged and kissed her, grabbed the letter and read it for herself.

The first person Rolivhuwa called was Khomisa. They spoke for over thirty minutes until Rolivhuwa's mother dished up supper. Usually Rolivhuwa's chores were cooking and dishing up. But that night she was 'exempted' from cooking.

Late in the evening after supper, before she washed the dishes, she sent an SMS to Mpho who called immediately.

'It's good to hear about the good news, Roli,' said Mpho. 'Let's talk tomorrow after knock-off time. Can I pick you up in front of McDonald's?'

'Thank you, *abuti* Mpho.'

So he wants to take me out again? Rolivhuwa mused as she put her cellphone down. *Or am I deluding myself about what could be a passing fancy of a romantic guy? Does Mpho really like me and can this liking graduate to the next stage ... should I expect something rosy to come out of this as Grace once said?*

* * *

An hour before knock-off, Rolivhuwa kept glancing at her cellphone to check the time, which seemed to be crawling at a snail's pace. A minute earlier her cellphone signalled an incoming message. She smiled, expecting rosy news, but instead she read: *Hi Roli, owing to an unexpected meeting with the President, I won't make it for today's appointment. Sori neh! Mpho.* Sorely disappointed, she re-read the SMS. She was relieved that she had not breathed a word to Khomisa about the possible outing with Mpho.

She played her cards close to her chest. If she had shared the potentially rosy news with anyone, how was she to explain why the meeting would not take place? A pessimistic person would paint a picture of Mpho and another tart smooching on the back seat of his BMW. Her mind would run riot and then magnify the problem.

That night as she put her head on her pillow she comforted herself by replaying a rosy thought when she was with Mpho during the derby in the executive suite, when he later high-fived her and even slapped her shoulder! But she said to herself, *Let me not be too hasty to disclose my wishes and fantasies and be disappointed soon when it happens to be just a passing fancy of a romantic guy.*

For the rest of the week what helped her to easily switch her thought from Mpho was packing her bags for her journey to UCT. That Friday her cellphone rang and she smiled when she realised that the caller was Mpho. She rushed out of the office.

'Tell me, Roli, when are you leaving for Cape Town?' Mpho inquired after exchanging greetings.

'The middle of the week after next.'

'So you are going to spend the last two weeks in Mamelodi?'

'Yes, *abuti* Mpho.'

'And this must be your last day as our volunteer.'

'It's alright if you …'

'Listen, I must have dinner with you tomorrow evening, is that okay?'

'Of course!'

When she returned to her desk, Khomisa grinned at her. 'Who were you speaking to? *Abuti* Mpho?'

Rolivhuwa giggled. 'I can't lie to you, my friend.'

'Surely this is more than just liking, Roli.'

'Some issues of life should be received with the head than with the heart.'

'What do you really want to tell me?'

'If you hastily take some things too seriously you end up heart-broken like a glass thrown from the tenth floor building.'

'I'll pray that the glass should not break.'

30

If there is time for everything under the sun, Rolivhuwa thought, *what is the season for me? To sow seeds of a new relationship, or will I have to wait again for a rosy season that seems to delay?*

Rolivhuwa was resting her chin on the heels of her hands with her elbows firmly planted on the dinner table at The Willows restaurant. Dinner was over and the sweetness of dessert had been washed down by tea.

'Let's go and sit over there on that park bench,' said Mpho after tipping the waiter.

Mpho leaned comfortably on the park bench, brushed his bald head, scratched his pitch-black beard and smiled. 'You know, Roli, I'm compelled to value you more because you won't be with us for months.'

'Thanks, *abuti* Mpho, I really appreciate.'

'And I want to put on record that I value you a lot. You are in fact of special value to me.'

'Of special value to you?'

'Yes.'

'It's less than a month that we've met, and now you …'

'But I have seen you before, Roli.'

'Where?'

'At your high school; the day you were performing *Hamba Sugar Daddy*.'

'Is that so? Why didn't I see you?'

'I tried to attract your attention but you had no time for me.'

Rolivhuwa chortled. 'I don't think you mean what you are saying.'

'Why?'

'You want to suggest that I was somebody and you were a nobody.'

'Well, you were an important actress while I was an ordinary member of the audience.'

'Okay. Did you like the sketch?'

'A lot.'

'Please tell me more.'

'Apart from excellent acting, I like the awareness it is raising. And it is also entertaining.'

'I am so pleased to hear about this positive feedback.'

He kept eye contact with her while he put his arm

on her arm. 'So, because I've seen you before, it was or it is easy for me to like you.'

Her face broke into a smile. 'Just to like me?'

'Well, let me say, it's more than liking. A special kind of liking.'

She smiled. 'What are you talking about now?'

'I told you that I'm compelled to value you more because you won't be with us for months. So, the thing I have hesitated to tell you, I will have to tell you now.'

She bent her neck until she touched his shoulder with her ear. 'I'm all ears.'

'I have to tell you that I ...' he faltered, 'I ... I love you Roli.'

She gasped. 'Really, Mpho?'

She had for the first time omitted '*abuti*'.

'I was hard with myself, Roli. I tried to pretend that I had no tender feelings towards you.'

He bent his neck and kissed her cheek.

She sighed and looked him deep into his eyes. 'Thank you, Mpho.'

He brushed her arm before he slipped his hand into hers.

She turned towards him. 'This is too good to be true. I can't believe that such a gorgeous guy like you can live without having a lot of young girls as his toys.

Tell me, Mpho, am I the only one or …?'

'You better believe you are the only one.'

'Just to comfort myself? And feel good?'

'We call that trust, the foundation of a sound relationship.'

With tearful eyes she looked at her hands and then at the stars, as if saying, *Our new love, the sky is the limit!*

She bent her neck and covered her face with her palms and raised her head a moment later wiping away a tear.

'This is too good to be true, Mpho.'

He squeezed her hand and brushed her arms towards her elbow and then squeezed her hand again.

'Let's go Roli. We'll have a lot to talk about for many days to come.'

She wiped a tear as she stood up and walked hand-in-hand with him.

* * *

When she arrived at home she never hesitated to send Khomisa an SMS: *Thank you for your prayer, Khomi. Do you remember what you once promised, I'll pray that the glass should not break?*

Within seconds her cellphone rang; it was Khomisa's call.

'Are you in love with Mpho? I told you that …' said a shrill voice.

Rolivhuwa burst into loud peals of laughter.

'I told you, Roli, that Mpho likes you. Now he loves you, lucky girl!'

Rolivhuwa continued to laugh. 'Thanks for your prayers, Khomi.'

'Why were you hiding this important news?'

'Khomi, do you remember what I once told you, before you promised to pray for me? Didn't I say that I don't want to be hasty to talk about my emotional matters? I wasn't hiding, my friend, I just preferred to wait and see how things developed. As I realised that Mpho was getting more interested, I kept saying to myself, *Let me not be too hasty to disclose my wishes and fantasies and be disappointed soon when it happens to be just a passing fancy of a romantic guy.*'

'Now you'll soon be cooing in the arms of that romantic guy, lucky girl!'

They laughed aloud.

* * *

Rolivhuwa went to sleep after midnight because she stayed up talking on her cellphone with Mpho, most of the time laughing loudly. She was sitting on her bed, leaning against the head-board, when she heard her mother saying, 'Vhovho, when are you going to sleep?'

Before she went to sleep she walked to the dressing mirror suppressing a laughter of victory. Victory because she had snatched Mpho out of the hands of a bevy of beautiful girls. With tears shining in her eyes she looked at her face in the mirror.

'Roli,' she addressed herself, 'You are blessed ... I mean truly blessed. Not by lustful rich old men but by,' she pointed heavenward. 'Thank You Lord for answering my prayer and Khomi's prayer. Thank You that my wishes and fantasies have been rewarded and I am not disappointed, but I am ecstatic that they did not turn into a passing fancy of a romantic guy. I will soon enjoy his million kisses and rest my head on his shoulder, drunk with love, Hallelujah! Halle-loo-looloo-jah! Amen.'

31

After unpacking half of her luggage in her room at the UCT's Graça Machel women's residence, she sent an SMS to Mpho. *Arrived safely in Cape Town. Sharing a room with a Nigerian student, Olayinka Adebayo. Want to have a nap for an hour. Tons of love, Roli.*

Her past few days had been hectic. Packing, seemingly endless conversations with her mother until midnight, face-to-face and cellphone conversations with Khomisa, falling in love with Mpho and going out with him, were all like a burden she could not deal with at that moment. But it felt like a huge load had fallen off her shoulders. About her roommate, her prayers had been answered: she prayed that she would share a room with a fellow Christian, not an 'ill-mannered' girl who smoked and would try to impose her values on her.

Mpho called in the evening after dinner as she unpacked the rest of the luggage. He spoke to her for almost an hour. She also called her mother and Khomisa.

In addition to getting used to the university – it's architecture, the lecturing staff, other students of different colours and African countries, the shuttle bus schedule – she had to get used to how Olayinka, whom she later addressed simply as Yinka, pronounced English words. At first when Yinka pronounced 'walk' as something that sounded like 'work' she laughed at herself for not being quick to understand her African sister. She was also amused when Yinka spoke pidgin words such as, 'Please-o, Welcome-o, Yes-o and I don't care-o!' She was also impressed with Yinka's confidence when she said, 'No be big problem. I go manage!' She also learned the first exclamation in Igbo, *Chi m o!* which means, My God! The fact that they were both first-year students assisted to their bonding.

One weekend six weeks later she was in the shuttle bus to main campus when she found herself cupping her mouth, out of embarrassment, when her eyes landed on a male student who reminded her of Mpho; like Mpho, the man was bald-headed with a lush black beard.

It's good to be away from him so that he should get some breathing space, she mused. *If our love won't survive a long distance, then so be it; I don't have to mourn its death. If, however, our love passes the test of distance and time, then it's good news. Perhaps, if I am next to him then I would see things that could perhaps make me miserable ... So, let it be out of sight, out of mind for these few months. I hope we'll miss each other and find our love renewed.*

One day as she strolled to the library she saw a bird soaring upwards. *May our love do likewise,* she expressed an ardent wish. She had plenty of excuses to send SMSes and inquire about how things were going with the supporters' coordinator's team and about how the club was performing, but she decided to focus on her studies. She was impressed with how the UCT library was open seven days a week, and only closed at 10pm. She was a member of the Students Christian Movement and she met other believers once a week on Fridays. Time moved fast and before she knew it was June holidays.

* * *

Owing to a hectic life at varsity and because of her passion for her studies, time moved fast and before she knew it was the end of the year. Her relationship with Mpho thrived and both admitted that distance was an opportunity rather than a threat, something they, being knowledgeable in marketing, learned from the SWOT – Strengths, Weaknesses, Opportunities and Threats – analysis.

She had earned a stipend as a library casual worker and she had part of her bursary for living expenses; as a result she was content with life – living within her budget and suppressing any appetite for expensive tastes.

When she observed how some of the girls maintained an expensive lifestyle by being blessees, she felt like shouting, 'No, *sistah* stop throwing your dignity out of the window in exchange for being showered with money and gifts by men who are old enough to be your fathers or grandfathers! No, that's not pure honey, but honey laced with poison!' She knew that when she returned to Mamelodi she would be an anti-blessee activist of some sort.

Whenever Mpho took her out and he paid for the bills, she was often quick to open her hand-bag, in a futile attempt to share the expenses. She had vowed that never would she again be sugar-daddied.

Noting her sensitivity regarding outing expenses, Mpho once joked, 'Is it a strength, an opportunity or a threat to me?'

'If you don't see it as a threat then it's your strength,' said Rolivhuwa.

They had a good laugh.

He squeezed her hand, bent his head toward her and they exchanged tender kisses.

Epilogue

That Friday at 2pm Rolivhuwa drove into the yard of Solomon Mahlangu High, and parked a brand-new yellow Citroën C1 City Slicker, with 'Sponsored by Motsepe Foundation' in bright green on both sides. As she switched off the ignition her cellphone registered an incoming WhatsApp message. It was from Mpho: *Hi Roli, Sori I will be late owing to unforeseen circumstances. But I will be there 2 B ur cheerleader. C U later.*

A moment later classrooms ejected thousands of boys and girls, wearing blue and yellow school uniforms. Loud noises and bursts of laughter filled the place.

She suddenly removed her hand from the steering wheel and put it on her mouth, as if she was trying to stifle laughter. She realised that she was in fact grinning as she recalled how two years ago she smilingly said to Kedibone with an open palm, '*Chomi ya ka*, please lend me another five rand, so that I should buy *sphatlo*.'

Rolivhuwa had passed her second year BCom with Bs in all courses, and she was planning to study for a third year.

She was there as an invited guest and speaker for the seminar titled, 'Choose life and live your dream'. The Mamelodi Pastors' Forum had established a welfare organisation to address the many challenges facing the girls. One of the pastors, who was once a blesser, was the one who came up with the idea of one-day workshops to be conducted at various high schools in Mamelodi. She would use the car – which was hers during the holidays – to visit selected high schools. The alumni, members of the community and the media had been invited.

She had prepared thoroughly for the seminar by reading Dr Myles Munroe's *The Principles and Power of Vision*, and Darryl Brister's *Living the Dream*. She was very confident about her attire: a gold and green ankle-length Nigerian print with matching head-gear which left part of her intricately braided hair protruding and tapering towards her nape. Her neck was adorned with a bead-strap which was a gift from her first-year roommate, Olayinka Adebayo.

For a moment she engaged in the visualisation technique she was fond of, to rehearse her presentation. She pictured herself in front of an enthusiastic audience who applauded as she presented her motivational speech. The sequence was interrupted by a girl wearing a blazer with a badge on the pocket that said, 'Head Prefect,' above the school motto, *Aim at the Stars*.

The learner led her to the entrance of the auditorium where the headmistress, four officials from the Department of Education, the teachers and members of the Mamelodi Pastors' Forum, were waiting as the girls entered. Her former teacher and counsellor, Ms Legodi, rushed to her, gave her a big hug, kissed her and led her by her hand and introduced her to the headmistress. Rolivhuwa waved to a group of teachers before she also shook hands with ten pastors.

Thirty minutes later, Ms Legodi, the programme director, stood up as soon as the headmistress, teachers, the pastors and the officials took their seats.

'On behalf the officials of the Department of Education, Mamelodi Pastors' Forum, alumnus Rolivhuwa Ramabulana, the headmistress, the staff, alumni, members of the community and the female learners, it affords me great pleasure to welcome you to this important seminar titled, 'Choose life and live your dream'. We at Solomon Mahlangu High pride ourselves on the fact that Ms Ramabulana is the product of,' at that moment she raised her hands and looked at them, 'our hands!'

Applause broke out.

'The purpose of this seminar is to sensitise our girls regarding certain life issues and challenges and to help them cope, through the motivation and guidance of role models and icons. The leadership at this institution is confident that they have made the best decision by inviting Ms Ramabulana as the seminar's guest speaker. Ms Ramabulana was one of our illustrious students who was a dramatist and activist two years ago. She passed Grade 12 with three distinctions.' The audience clapped their hands. 'She is currently a BCom Accounting student and has passed her second year with no less than B symbols. This year she will do her third year and complete next year.' The audience applauded. 'Over to you, Ms Ramabulana.'

As Rolivhuwa scanned the audience she saw Mpho, Khomisa and her mother taking their seats at the back. Their presence triggered off adrenalin which she had harnessed to her advantage.

'Did you know that planet earth has seven billion people? And did you know that these seven billion people can be divided into three groups?'

She paused 'What are these three groups? Those who make things happen, those who watch things happen, and those who don't know what's happening.'

Ms Legodi led the applause.

'Did you know that you are where you are today because of yesterday's thoughts?'

Rolivhuwa smiled at her audience. 'Yes, you are where you are today because of yesterday's thoughts. Your actions followed your thoughts. This brings me to today's topic: 'Choose life and live your dream'.

'I like the order of the words in this topic: If you want to live your dream, if you want to achieve your dream, you must first make the right choice; you must choose life. This means that if you choose death you'll not be able to realise your dream.

'Can people choose death? Yes. They do so without realising it. When you are an infant and a child, your parents take care of you. If you pick up a bottle full of poison, they will take it from you and remove you from the poisonous thing. But there comes a time when you must make your own choices. You make a choice about the type of friends you associate with and the type of relationships you have. No one will force you to choose friends and no one will compel you to choose a boyfriend or *le-ghintsha,* a young man who makes a living by criminal activities such as car theft.

'When the Children of Israel entered the Promised Land they first had to fight and defeat the giants. They could not do anything ... they could not till the land, eat the crops and drink wine while giants were moving about. No. First they had to deal with the giants.

'We are in democratic South Africa, which is a sort of a Promised Land. We are blessed ... I truly mean it. We are blessed compared to our parents who were burdened by apartheid. We are called born-frees who have to make the right choices in order to defeat the giants. We have to choose: follow our heads or hearts; our choices are what we sow now and reap later.

'If we are going to talk about giants as girl children, we have to talk about the elephant in the room, and that is about sugar daddies and blessers. This topic appears in print and electronic media, including YouTube. Names of celebs – young women involved with sugar daddies – come and go. Yesterday it was Khanyi, today it's Amanda and tomorrow it will be another young woman in search of fame or wealth.

'Now let's talk statistics.' She smiled to her audience as she continued, 'Did you know that according to the statistics by social researchers, 14 to 21 percent of girls at tertiary institutions have sugar daddy relationships? This figure is fast increasing because, according to the Blessfinder website, the demand for blessers is so high that it does not have enough blessers for the thousands of blessees active on its site every day. Why do they become blessees? To put it bluntly – why do they take part in transactional sex?'

'There are three main reasons. 'One! For money! Two! For gifts! And Three! For good grades! Yes good grades! For some of these students, the way to a graduation ceremony is through the lecturers' or professors' bedrooms! My roommate at UCT is a Nigerian girl, Olayinka Adebayo. She said that her uncle, who is a professor of English at a Nigerian university, told her that often some female students opened their thighs for him during lectures because they desperately wanted to pass the language, which is compulsory in some degrees. So, please don't be part of these statistics.

'Now let's talk about the consequences: One. STIs – Sexually transmitted infections. Two. HIV/AIDS. Three. Teenage pregnancies. According to statistics from the Department of Basic Education, 99 000 school girls fell pregnant during 2013. Please do not be part of these sorry statistics. Four. Death from botched illegal abortions. To say more about abortions: I become sad and angry when I see leaflets pasted on walls and electricity lamp posts all over the township, written, "Abortion – safe and pain free". Are we a nation that makes business for some unscrupulous people who are cashing in on this unfortunate situation?'

Applause.

'Five. Some blessees are often attacked by blessers' wives and relatives. For example, South Africa's blessee number one, the woman who has been on the tip of everyone's tongue, Thoko, was severely assaulted, her weave was pulled out and she was left nursing a black eye. So you can see that people reap what they sow; if you choose to be a blessee you will get your reward. Your actions will follow your thoughts, your choice.'

'The sixth reason why you must say no to blessers is that you can be turned into an overnight prostitute and a drug mule. If you are desperate for money and status and you are on the hunt to get blessed, you can easily be tricked into prostitution and drug dealing. And what happens to a drug mule? She serves a long prison sentence or faces a death sentence.

'The seventh reason: Human trafficking. Many young girls are not aware that their so-called blessers are actively involved in turning them in to human traffickers.'

'The eighth and last reason is emotional and physical abuse. It's not smooth sailing all the time on the blesser–blessee boat. During stormy seasons you can be physically and emotionally abused by a blesser who may be experiencing financial problems; some who become broke can be irritable and can be jealous and begin to say, "So you want to leave me because I'm not giving you money and nice things as I used to?" As a result this kind of a blesser can turn a blessee into a punching bag.'

'Having mentioned the eight reasons why you must say no to sugar daddies and blessers, the choice is yours: you can choose life or death.'

She paused and scanned her audience. 'I am going to be vulnerable because I am going to talk about my past, which was partly a mess because of my choices.' She looked in the direction of Ms Legodi. 'Ma'am Legodi knows what I'm talking about. I am from there and I know what I'm talking about. I am writing a book to be entitled, *Confessions of a Former Blessee*.

'I have learnt from my mistakes. I had to make a choice: to remain in a blessee–blesser relationship or quit and face the consequences. I quit and I was faced with life-threatening challenges, where I could easily lose my life. I had to make a choice: to choose a friend who represented life and not death. Fortunately, my pain, stress and tears have compelled me to choose to follow God, who turned my lemons into lemonade and my tragedy into triumph!'

The audience applauded.

'So please make choices you won't regret later in life. Girls, some relationships are like inviting a hijacker onto your plane. And so, don't be surprised when you end up at a miserable destination. Never envy sugar babies and never wish you had what they have, for they pay a heavy price!'

The audience applauded.

'Girls, delay or defer gratification and focus on

your studies. For your studies are your mother and your father!'

The audience applauded.

'Those who wait never regret!'

The audience applauded.

'Those who wait often get handsome rewards!'

The audience applauded.

'When you are at university work hard. Remember the advice of our national icon and former President Mandela, "It may seem difficult but it can be done." Remember also the slogan of Mamelodi Sundowns, 'The sky is ...'

'The limit!' The audience completed.

'And remember the motto of our school ...'

'Aim at the Stars,' the audience responded.

'Our mothers and fathers, grandmothers and grandfathers were burdened with apartheid. You and me are "born-frees". So what are our excuses? You work hard to be admitted at a particular university and instead of doing what you have been sent there for, you just want the easy, cheap and immoral way out by sleeping through your degree? *Hawu*, come on girls, be serious!'

They applauded.

'So, don't ever think about doing bedroom-ology with your lecturer and professor in order to pass your degree. If you want fame and wealth you have to work hard and get a financially rewarding career. So, don't choose a dangerous short cut of opening your thighs to rich old men and university professors. How sad that we live in a society where our young girls are no longer dreaming of becoming social workers, lawyers, scientists, pharmacists and engineers but they think of the easy way of becoming blessees. *Haibo*! Prostitution has become trendy!'

They applauded.

'Before I go on with part two, which is living your dream, let me share this important information. What I have gone through has made me an activist. I am one of the anti-blesser activists who are organising a march, to be named #blessersmustfall', to the Union Buildings.'

Ms Legodi clapped her hands and others did likewise.

'And I am going to lead the march, and we ...'

Loud applause interrupted her.

'Yes, I am going to lead the march and we are going to hand a memorandum to the Minister of Women, Gender and Children. Part One of the programme will consist of poetry by women poets, music by women and a short drama, *Hamba Sugar Daddy*. The Minister of Health, Dr Aaron Motsoaledi has been invited and we expect him to announce details about the project his ministry has in mind. According to a newspaper report, the minister has announced a R3 billion plan to curb the spread of HIV by protecting girls and women aged between 15 and 24 from the increasing number of blessers.'

A pastor led the applause.

'This will be a three-year programme to wean young girls off sugar daddies. Now I'm encouraging all of you to take part in the march which will take place next month. After this seminar, during refreshments, a register will be circulated, and please write your names, addresses and cellphone numbers. Hash-Tag, blessers must,' at that juncture Rolivhuwa raised her fist and punched down, 'fall!'

A learner stood up raising her fist, 'Yes, blessers must fall!'

Loud applause broke out.

Another learner stood up raising her fist, 'Blessers must fall!'

Other girls responded, 'Blessers must fall!' They clapped their hands rhythmically shouting out several times, 'Blessers must fall!'

Everybody in the auditorium rose to their feet, chanting, 'Blessers must fall!'

Rolivhuwa raised her hands and the people cheered as they sat down.

'I so wish we can march straight to the Union Building now!'

The audience applauded lustily.

Rolivhuwa paused as she scanned the audience with a winsome smile. 'Now let me speak about living your dream. The great men and women who inspire this nation all agree that the poorest man or woman in the world is the man or woman without a dream. Not the man without money, but the man without a dream.

'Why is having a dream important? Having a dream will keep you focused. If you don't have a dream anyone can take you anywhere. If you are travelling with people and you see them alighting at a certain station, you must remain in the train for you know where you are going.'

Rolivhuwa saw Mpho and Khomisa at the back nodding and smiling.

'According to Darryl Brister, dreams are visual manifestations of our purpose; they are seeds planted in the soil of our imaginations. The key word is 'Purpose'. What is purpose? Purpose is the reason something was made. Girls, this is very important; so, let me repeat: Purpose is the reason something was made. Every manufacturer produces a product to fulfil a specific purpose, and every product is designed with the ability to fulfil this purpose. I repeat: Every product is designed with the ability to fulfil this purpose.

'The purpose of a seed is, for example, to produce trees. Girl child, what is your purpose? Perhaps your purpose is to be a pharmaceutical scientist who should discover an AIDS drug, but why have you chosen to abort your purpose by using your body to satisfy the lust of a rich old man?'

They applauded.

'What happens if you don't understand the purpose of a particular tool? You won't appreciate it and you can therefore abuse it. What will you think if you see a man using a fork he's been eating with to dig in the garden? You'll think he's lost his mind. This is what's happening when young girls are using their bodies to satisfy the blessers' lust. They should be using their bodies as athletes, dancers, actors, motivational speakers and so on. Girl child, use your youth and energy for yourself and not against yourself.'

A girl led the applause.

Rolivhuwa gestured towards the girl. 'Thank you for your enthusiasm!'

Rolivhuwa grinned. 'Two months ago during a colloquium regarding the blesser–blessee phenomenon at UCT, a fellow student who is from Khayelitsha read this line which I requested from him, "Yellow bone, were you born to be bang-banged by blessers?" I hope we all know what a yellow bone is; it's a light complexioned girl.'

'Now let me share with you some tips about how you can realise your dream – how to live your dream. Broadly speaking, you should have a plan: the saying goes that if you fail to plan you are planning to fail. I repeat: if you fail to plan you are planning to fail. You are like a contractor who is trying to construct a building without a blueprint.

'Step one: Eliminate distractions

'Sit down somewhere by yourself, away from distractions, and allow yourself some uninterrupted time to think and develop your plan.

'Step two: Write down your goals

'Every person alive should have goals. In the next three or five to ten years from now, what do you want to accomplish? Whatever goals you want to achieve, put them down on paper. The process of physically writing down your goals helps you to crystallise them in your mind. It also helps you to commit to them.

'Here is an interesting fact: A Harvard Business School study once found that:

i. 3 per cent of the population record their goals in writing;
ii. 14 per cent have goals but don't write them down, whereas
iii. 83 per cent do not even have clearly defined goals.

'A more interesting fact: This 3 per cent earned ten times more than the 83 per cent group! The question is: Are you part of the top 3 per cent who make things happen or are you part of the 83 per cent, who watch things happen or don't even know what's happening?

'Step three: Look at your goals every day

'If you paste your written goals on the fridge or next to your mirror you make them more real in your mind. This can help you become focused so that you can ultimately realise your dream.

'Step four: Speak to yourself about your dream

'Speak to yourself about your dream; experts on motivation call it affirmation. First, say to yourself: "By this year ... I want to achieve ...' Secondly, when, for example, you are still training to be a beauty therapist, look at yourself in the mirror every morning and in the evening and say to yourself, 'Hallo beauty therapist!' This will help you stay focused and keep you on track when you are facing challenges.

'Step five: Create deadlines

'Without deadlines, your goals are mere wishes. Certain things should be done by a certain date. Set deadlines for both short-term and long-term goals. Remember that deadlines can be flexible. Life changes and so do goals. So never be afraid to adjust the time frame for a goal. What's important is to keep moving.

'Step six: Dare to be different

'If you expect your dream to come true, you must dare to be different. You were not born to be just anyone else. You don't have to be part of the clique. If girls in your street or section are having babies before they are 18 and you are 20, don't cave in to persuasion and peer pressure. If most girls choose IT and marketing and you desire to be a pilot, go for it. And don't be paralysed by excu-sitis or status-quo-titis. I repeat, don't be paralysed by excu-sitis or status-quo-titis. Get out of your comfort zone and run with your dream!

'Step seven: Hang around successful people

'There are three types of minds: Great minds, average minds and small minds. Great minds discuss ideas, average minds focus on events and small minds discuss people. If you are an eagle but you scratch around with chickens you will fly as high as the hens. If you hang around achievers, the movers and shakers, the history makers, they will infect you to be like them. Good company will nourish and uplift your dream while bad company will corrupt and destroy it. AND FINALLY:

'Step eight: Don't give up on your dream

'Many people fail because they give up the first time they fall down. When your dream takes longer to come true or there are obstacles, do not give up on your dream. Girl child, you are too close to the finish line. You've come too far to turn back now. Winners aren't quitters. Remember Nelson Mandela's advice: 'It may seem difficult but it can be done.' If you are knocked down, tell your problem, "If you knock me down, I am going to get up again. And I'm going to get up until you are tired of knocking me down!"'

Applause.

'Girls of Mtubatuba, please dream big. If you just choose to open your thighs to lustful rich old men you are thinking smaller than beetles, and you are abusing your purpose. Why don't you aspire to be like many young women who are role models, such as a lecturer and PhD candidate, Thulile Khanyile, who has won a Department of Science and Technology "Women in Science" award?'

A learner led the applause.

'Let me hasten to correct the generalisation. Ninety-something per cent of the Mtubatuba girls are good girls who have a promising future.'

Rolivhuwa paused and breathed in with a smile. 'Girl child, the future is in your hands. Our parents have given us the baton; let's not throw it away, but let's run with it and do what we have been purposed to do. Born-free, you were born to fly high, for the sky is your limit, baby! Girls, please say after me: "The future is in our hands!"'

'The future is in our hands!' said the girls in unison.

'So I must equip myself to make a contribution ...' said Rolivhuwa.

'So I must equip myself to make a contribution ...' the girls shouted.

'To the economic freedom of my generation.'

'To the economic freedom of my generation.'

'Being a young South African means that ...'

'Being a young South African means that ...'

'The challenges are mine to fix.'

'The challenges are mine to fix.'

Ms Legodi led the applause this time.

'Without planning, without identifying and pursuing our dreams and without relevant skills, the youth of today will be remembered for being blessees, for criminal activities, for protests and destruction of property.'

'So choose life and live your dream. I thank you.'

The audience rose to their feet and clapped their hands, cheered and whistled.

'Roli! Roli! Roli!' some learners cheered.

Ms Legodi bared her palms to Rolivhuwa; the two high-fived and hugged.

'Well done, Roli!' said Ms Legodi.

'Thank you, Ma'am!'

'There's no doubt that ...'

Ms Legodi was interrupted by Mpho who hugged and kissed Rolivhuwa. Khomisa high-fived Rolivhuwa and they exchanged hugs and kisses. In a moment Rolivhuwa was surrounded by the headmistress, education department officials, teachers, pastors, and other people filing up in a queue – all wanting a slice of her time to congratulate her. Rolivhuwa felt a hand tapping her.

'*Comi ya ka!*' someone shouted.

When Rolivhuwa turned she saw Kedibone, her former classmate and erstwhile fellow blessee. 'I'll see you later Kedi,' said Rolivhuwa.

A group of learners waited behind people chatting to Rolivhuwa. The inner circle of well-wishers comprised Ms Legodi, the headmistress, an official from the Department of Education, the chairman of the Mamelodi pastor's forum and three pastors.

'We should organise the youth from all our churches to attend the next seminar,' said one of the pastors.

'This seminar should be replicated in all districts of the province,' said the education official.

'Okay, let's discuss this over refreshments,' said Ms Legodi.

After the refreshments, when Rolivhuwa returned from the toilet she found a group of girls waiting for her. They had just written their particulars in the #blessersmustfall march register. She gave all the girls quick hugs.

Suddenly, one girl shouted, 'Blessers must fall!' Other girls also toyi-toyied, chanting, 'Blessers must fall!' Six girls tore pages from their notebooks, created mini-placards and wrote:

Blessers must fall
Phanzi with blessers
Blessees, R U proud of a shame?
Blessees, wrong can't B right
Arrest the bastards!
Let 'em go 2 jail

'Girls, I like your spontaneity, creativity and energy,' said Rolivhuwa gleaming with a smile.

While Rolivhuwa was the girls' cheerleader, clapping rhythmically, she felt someone touching her shoulder. 'Sis Roli, my mother wants to meet you,' said a girl who could have been only about fourteen.

'Who's your mother?' Rolivhuwa asked.

'Mma-Masemola,' said the girl.

Bigvy's wife wants to meet me? Rolivhuwa thought as she followed the girl to a thick-set woman whose face looked like she was recovering from *dichubaba*, the facial marks, wearing a smart bluish two-piece suit. For a moment her mind went to that scene with Bigvy, when he had said, *My wife said: "I'm going to mutilate the vagina of that bitch!"* For a moment she was in fight-or-flight mode but she composed herself; she was relieved when she saw a gentle smile crossing the woman's face.

'I'm Mma-Masemola,' said the woman, who grinned as she extended her hand.

'I'm Rolivhuwa.'

'I heard a lot about you, Roli.'

She felt like asking, *Heard about me from who? Bigvy?* 'Really?'

'Yes. I heard about the good work you are doing in our community.'

'Thank you, Mma-Masemola.'

'Keep up the good work, my girl.'

'Thank you, Mma-Masemola.'

'And remain a good role model.'

'Thank you Mma ...'

'Good-bye, Roli.'

'Bye!'

Rolivhuwa felt a hand touching hers. Bigvy's daughter stood beside her with a coy smile.

'I want you to be my friend, sis Roli.'

'Surely? No problem. What's your name?'

'Pontsho.'

'Nice to meet you, Pontsho. I'm sure I can make time to speak to you over a cup of tea.'

'Thank you, sis Roli.'

Rolivhuwa smiled as she studied her face, not knowing what to discuss with her former blesser's daughter.

'And how's your dad?' Rolivhuwa probed unintentionally.

'Papa is lying on a hospital bed.'

'Hospital bed? Is he sick?'

'Yes, he has a kidney problem. And he's passing urine through a plastic pipe.'

'I'm sorry to hear about that. Tell him I wish him a speedy recovery.'

'I will. I'm sure he'll appreciate your visit.'

'Okay. I'll have to make time.'

For a moment a naughty thought crossed Rolivhuwa's mind. *So I'm going to be Bigvy's emotional blesser and he'll be the blessee!* As Pontsho walked to her mother Rolivhuwa felt a hand tapping her shoulder. It was Mpho's hand.

'I'm sorry, Mpho. Hope you don't feel neglected.'

'No problem Roli.'

'Please come and meet my mom,' Rolivhuwa took Mpho's arm and led him to her mother.

'Mama, meet Mpho Maleka, my ... my friend.'

Mpho and her mother exchanged handshakes.

'I'm glad to meet you, Mr Maleka.'

'Pleased to meet you, Mama,' said Mpho.

'He's the marketing officer of Mamelodi Sundowns Football Club. He's the new man in my life.'

Her mother grinned. 'It's wonderful, Vhovho.'

Rolivhuwa thought, *Mother, I hope you'll now stop thinking that I can go back to Bigvy.*

* * *

Rolivhuwa and Mpho were inseparable. They attended football matches and sat in the executive suites hand-in-hand or cuddling each other's waists. She invited him to her church and introduced him to her pastor; he reciprocated. One weekend during Miss Mamelodi Sundowns' pageant they were both judges. They also ate out a lot at many restaurants. All these activities conduced to a thriving love relationship.

* * *

'I want you to spend next year at UCT as a married woman, with my diamond wedding ring shining on your ...' said Mpho as he touched her ring finger that night during a candle-lit dinner at Mafikizolo restaurant.

They were sitting at a table holding hands and hungry for intimacy, which was accentuated by the romantic soft string music.

Rolivhuwa gasped.

'Yes,' Mpho added, 'I don't want those Xhosa boys to take food out of my mouth.'

She chuckled. 'Thank you, Mpho.'

They turned to each other, squeezed each other's hands, tilted their heads towards each other and savoured a few unhurried kisses.

* * *

Se mo tšere-tšere senatla,
Se mo tšere-tšere senatla,
Se mo tšere-tšere senatla,
Ngwana o tšerwe ke senatla,
Heyta, mapantsola hulle moenie worrie,
Ngwana o tšerwe ke senatla.

The popular township wedding song went on repeatedly. The bride, Rolivhuwa, wearing a snow-white wedding dress and the groom, Mpho, in a tight-fitting cream-white Chinese-collared suit, were at the front of two rows of bridesmaids and groomsmen.

They were tap-dancing forward and side-ways, according to the rhythm of the song sung with great enthusiasm, between throngs of onlookers – their families, friends and other well-wishers – who had formed a guard of honour. Some relatives were cheering in the style of the Bapedi tribespeople, chanting, *'Howaa! Howaa!'* and *'Li-li-li-li!'* From the tent pitched on the lawn in front of the house, Aunt Bertha emerged holding a gourd from which she scooped and then threw at the couple's faces, sorghum corn which served as African confetti ...

In the next scene the bridal procession was in one of the main streets in the township on the left lane, guided by the metropolice on motorbikes flashing blue lights. Suddenly a procession appeared in the opposite direction. Rolivhuwa gasped when she saw a huge portrait of Bigvy displayed on the side of the hearse with letters on top, 'Rest In Peace.' Rolivhuwa waved at the hearse saying, *Hamba Sugar Daddy, to your final destination; you have reaped what you've sowed!*

As the hearse drove past her it veered off the road and hit a tree. The coffin fell out and smashed against the tarmac and when it fell apart Bigvy glided out feet first, sat on his haunches, squatted, stood on his feet and walked towards Rolivhuwa; he was wearing a jet-black suit, his eyes covered by dark sunglasses. Utterly terrified, she shrieked, trying to break loose from Mpho, to run away but he held her tightly. At an arm's length from her Bigvy opened his arms ready to embrace her, bared soot-black teeth, saying with a hoarse voice, 'Roli my apple-tart I'm still in love with you – Dr Motsoaledi or not; so, let's continue from where …' Rolivhuwa screamed with all the air in her lungs.

There was a loud knocking on the door of Rolivhuwa's bedroom.

'Vhovho!' her mother continued to knock, 'What's happening? Is there an intruder?' A further knock. 'Please open!'

Rolivhuwa rose from her bed, realising that she had had a nightmare which started off as a rosy and sweet dream. She was reminded of what Khomisa once said to her, that enjoying the benefits of being a blessee was like taking honey laced with poison.

THE END

Glossary
(in alphabetical order)

Aiwa: (tshiVenda) No
Aowa: (Sepedi/North Sesotho) No
Ausi: Elder sister
Bafana ba Style: Mamelodi Sundowns Football Club
Bra: A shortened form of 'brother'; respectful prefix to male names
Buwa sebuwi, buwaa!: Speak speaker, speak!
Chomi ya ka: (urban Sesotho-based lingo) My friend
Hamba: (Nguni languages) Go (away)
Le ja soft: (Township slang) (literally: you are eating soft) You are living comfortably
Lira: Performing name of Lerato Molapo a South Africa's top female soul artist
Lot's wife: See Bible, Genesis 19: 26
Lotto: Money from the betting for the Lottery fund
Mahala: Free of charge
Malana le dikilana, ditlhogwana le maotwana: Chicken intestines, stomach, liver, head and feet. Consuming these items are often viewed by some people as living below middle-class levels.
Mamazala: (Nguni languages) Mother-in-law
Mamfundisi: (Nguni languages) Pastor's wife

Manga manga business: (Township lingo) Monkey tricks
MEC: Member of the Executive Council (of the province)
Moegoe: Dunce, stupid person/rural person who can be easily exploited by city people
Mokhukhu: (Urban Sesotho) Shack
Mzalwane: Reborn Christian
NAFCOCI: National African Federation of Chamber of Commerce and Industries
Ntate: A respectful and formal way of addressing older males
Ntoto: Penis (Sepedi)
Phambili: Forward
Phanzi: Down (or away with)
Pasela: Gift to the buyer after the sale
SAPS: South African Police Service
Sefebe: Slut (Sesotho)
Se mo tšere- tšere …:
 The strong/muscular man has indeed snatched her,
 The strong/muscular man has indeed snatched her,
 The strong/muscular man has indeed snatched her,
 The girl has been snatched by the strong/muscular man,
 Heyta, mapantsola must not bother (about the girl)
 The girl has been snatched by the strong/muscular man.
Smallernyana: A Sesotho-fied emphasis of 'small'
Smatsatsa: Beautiful girl or woman
Sphatlo: (urban Sesotho-based lingo) a homemade sandwich made of a quarter loaf of white bread into which atchar, fried eggs, polony and other things as preferred by the buyer are inserted

STI: Sexually Transmitted Infection
Tokoloshe: Leprechaun-like evil and naughty being, referred to with humour as a 'short boy', believed in by many Africans
Tsotsi: Thug, criminal, guy with a concealed knife
Vela-ba-hleke: A charm which literally means, appear (and) they laugh
Voetsek: or Voertsek (Afrikaans) from 'voort se ek' literally, 'go, say I'; very rude remark
Wa lala wa sala: (Sesotho) (literally: you sleep, you remain behind) If you are unwise or not streetwise, you miss an opportunity
Wena: (Sesotho and Nguni languages including xiTsonga) You
Women's Day: Celebrated annually on 9 August (inspired by the 20 000 strong anti-apartheid women's march to the Union Buildings in 1956)

Acknowledgments

My heartfelt thanks to:

Dr Nkhelebeni Phaswana, the owner of Kalahari Publishers – for commissioning me to write this novel.

Jacana Media's Bridget Impey – for believing in me and cherishing enthusiasm in publishing the novel.

Jacana Media's team: production, editorial, marketing and supporting staff – for putting their industrious hands on the plough.

Journalists who have written articles about sugar daddies, blessers and blessees, which were published in print media such as *Drum* magazine, *Sowetan*, *City Press*, *Move*! and *The Sunday Independent* (Life Relationships).

SABC's Channel 404 – for broadcasting about blessers and blessees – to which Amanda Cele, 'SA Blessee Number 1,' many experts and researchers and Health Minister, Dr Aaron Motsoaledi and KwaZulu-Natal's Health MEC, Dr Sibongiseni Dhlomo, have contributed.

The late Dr Myles Munroe, whose book, *The Principles and Power of Vision*, I have consulted.

Dr John Tibane, whose book, *Advance Your Life*, I have consulted.

Pastor Darryl Brister, whose book, *Living the Dream*, I have consulted.

Pastor Rick Warren, whose book, *The Purpose Driven Life*, I have consulted.

Ms Busi-ka Mgiba, a Mamelodi-based poet, singer and activist – for sharing information about sugar babies and sugar daddies.

Ms Gwen Setalala, a high school educator – for sharing information about sugar babies and sugar daddies prevalence at high school.

Ms Zoleka Dlungana – for reminding me about and also singing with me, the popular wedding song, *Se mo tšere-tšere senatla*.

The unknown African composers of *Se mo tšere-tšere senatla*.

My wife, Sibongile – for her patience and kindness when I was present but absent at times owing to me attending to this manuscript.

My sons, Ramaswaile and Bafana-Bafana – for bearing with me when I was at times an absent father.

My daughter, Thabang, whose worldview as part of the young generation was handy in her capacity as another proof-reader.

And finally and most significantly:

My Creator, *Modimo, Ramatla-ohle, Makgona-tšohle*, for lending me the breath of life, and for blessing me with excellent health and wisdom. Hallelujah!

Author's Note

The writing of this novel has been a long yet rewarding journey, which started in 2012, initially as a small commissioned assignment. I welcomed the idea as an opportunity to venture out of my comfort zone and routine.

I decide to focus on the sugar daddy/sugar baby relationship, based on an article, 'A bitter taste of a sweet life', which was published in *Drum* magazine. I found the theme, the stories and circumstances of the girls involved exceedingly fascinating for a writing project, containing much social relevance.

The journey of a thousand miles began with the first step, as I sat on my desk, creating the protagonist who would be burdened with a problem and hurdles to jump over and be 'blessed' or rewarded at the end of going through hell.

Additional steps followed as I identified other characters. From the stories of the anonymous sugar babies I read, it was easy for me to identify the heroines' allies and enemies.

The initial project did not materialise, so I was enormously thrilled when Bridget Impey of Jacana Media showed enthusiasm about the novel. The title is the result of our brainstorming together and was chosen for its thematic relevance and intrigue. It was a rewarding experience to work through this project.

The birth-pangs and labour pains over, the umbilical cord cut and the baby, *Hamba Sugar Daddy*, now bouncing up and down the world stage, the beholder can be the judge and jury.